PROPERTY OF BIGFOOT

KINGS OF ANARCHY: NEW MEXICO
BOOK 1

CHRISTINE MICHELLE

christineandanne.com

Proofreading - Christy Sears
Editing - Anna Paige
https://annapaigewrites.com/

Paperback Edition

ABOUT THE BOOK
TRIGGER WARNINGS / AUTHOR'S
NOTES

Kings of Anarchy: New Mexico by Christine Michelle is part
of a multi-author, shared, motorcycle club romance world
brought to you by: Glenna Maynard and Morgan Jane
Mitchell.

PROPERTY OF BIGFOOT (Kings of Anarchy: New Mexico
Book 1)
*An age gap, single dad, obsessive/possessive relationship where she
rescues him and he falls first!*

Sammy
I had to stop and help.
There was no question in my mind that it was the right thing
to do, even after I noticed his one percent patch. The Kings of
Anarchy MC were notorious in my hometown.
Not only did I turn over the evidence to the club, but I drove
to the hospital and stayed to make sure Bigfoot would be
okay.
That started his obsession with me.

I wasn't sure about getting more involved with the club, or a single father who was decade older than me, but there was no denying he was irresistible.

Bigfoot
She took care of me on the side of the road.
She put my club's interests before her own and before the law.
It took me a while to even learn her name.
Then it took me even longer to convince Sammy to give me the time of day.
She worried about the club life, our age difference, my ex, and my kid. It was up to me to lay all her worries to rest.
There was never a doubt in my mind that my persistence would pay off. Sammy was mine from the moment our eyes first met on the side of that road. She just needed time to wrap her head around it.

TRIGGER WARNINGS

Everything!
Just kidding.

- Violence
- Death
- Murder
- Attempted Murder

- Accidental Murder
- Kidnapping
- Gun Running
- Alcohol & Drug references
- Sexual Situations
- Family Betrayal
- Car Accident/Motorcycle Accident
- Drug Dealing
- A brothel/whorehouse
- Strong language
- Dark humor
- Turned on by violence

Author's Notes

Violence, New Mexico is a fictional town located near where you might find Red Hill and Quemado, New Mexico on a real map. It is very close to the Arizona border on both sides of US-60.
Everything about this book is FICTION!

WELCOME TO THE KINGS OF ANARCHY
KOAMC CODE

Anarchy - Where the Kings rule in chaos

Respect the Mother Chapter
Your loyalty stays with your patch
Brotherhood above all
Never touch another brother's ol' lady
Ride or die, no questions asked
Never back down from a fight
Never let a brother ride solo
Each chapter sets its own damn rules

Nobody fucks with the Kings

KINGS OF ANARCHY MC
First run authors, book titles, and month of release:

GLENNA MAYNARD
Property of Hero - May 2023
Property of Big Daddy - April 2025
Property of Woods - June 2025

CHELSEA CAMARON
Property of Chux - March 2025

DARLENE TALLMAN
Property of Rio - March 2025

CHRISTINE MICHELLE
Property of Bigfoot - March 2025

MAX HENRY
Property of Chaos - April 2025

LIBERTY PARKER
Property of Indiana - April 2025

E.C. LAND
Property of Fire - April 2025

CLAIRE C. RILEY
Property of Bear - May 2025

JANINE INFANTE BOSCO
Property of Shotgun - May 2025

ANDI LYNN
Property of Mercy - May 2025

MANDA MELLET
Property of Saint - June 2025

AMY DAVIES
Property of Camo - June 2025

MORGAN JANE MITCHELL
Property of Legend - June 2025

WINTER TRAVERS
Property of Anchor - June 2025

NAOMI PORTER

x

Welcome to the Kings of Anarchy

Property of El Jefe - July 2025

SAPPHIRE KNIGHT

Property of Madman - July 2025

JESSA AARONS

Property of Rourke - July 2025

KRISTINE ALLEN

Property of Mako - July 2025

KATHLEEN KELLY

Property of Blade - August 2025

VERLENE LANDON

Property of Prowler - August 2025

RYAN MICHELE

Property of Thrasher - August 2025

NIKKI LANDIS

Property of Scythe - August 2025

JEANNE ST. JAMES

Property of Stone - Sept. 2025

BINK CUMMINGS

Property of Necro - September 2025

K.L. DONN

Property of Brute & Axl - September 2025

MADELINE SHEEHAN

Property of Nash - September 2025

MADALYN JUDGE

Property of Tacoma - October 2025

CARMEN JENNER

Property of Hawk - October 2025

M. MERIN

Property of Bull - October 2025

JORDAN MARIE

Property of Grifter - October 2025

NOBODY

FUCKS WITH

THE KINGS

1. CRASH AND BURN

SAMMY

I KNEW THE MINUTE THE EIGHTEEN-WHEELER FLEW AROUND ME ON US-60 that my night was about to take a turn for the worse.

We just rolled over the state line coming from Arizona into New Mexico when the asshole thought it would be fun to try to pass. Either he didn't realize there was a man on a Harley in front of me or he didn't care.

"Fuck!" I yelled into the empty cab of my truck as he blew by. The wind gust he kicked up rocked the hell out of my little Toyota Tacoma and made me wonder how that would feel to the Harley he was about to breeze by in the same way. I didn't have a moment to think about it. As he passed the motorcycle, one of his tires blew and the debris flew right into the biker.

I stepped on my brake and swerved off to the side of the road, thanking every deity known to man that there wasn't anyone else on the road at the time. I also thanked my "adopt a biker" mentality. The cushion of distance I kept between us was the only reason I didn't roll right over him.

The motorcycle took a direct hit from the debris, but I

thought the rider may have taken a large chunk to his side, as well. He flew off the bike and flipped in the air, which might have been a good thing, considering the way the motorcycle bucked up and came off the ground before it finally landed and slid over into the into some scrub brush at the side of the road.

The biker had been thrown backward as he was launched off the bike and slid to stop just in front of my truck when all was finally said and done. I couldn't even imagine what the impact had done to him, especially after taking a hit from the truck debris.

I was so thankful that I had eased off the gas when the truck tried to pass me. Had I not, the biker would have ended up in my windshield or under my tires. Neither of those options were good for me. The trucker kept on trucking like his tire never blew out, like he hadn't just taken out a motor-cyclist.

My irrational anger almost got the best of me. Instead, I threw my hazard lights on, grabbed my phone, and jumped out of my truck to go check on the biker before calling 9-1-1, so I could let them know whether to send an ambulance or a clean-up crew with the police. When I reached the man, he groaned and tried to sit up, but I stopped him with a firm hand on his shoulder.

"Please, don't try to move. You don't know what could be injured and you might make everything worse," I explained. He moaned but laid back down as I asked questions. "I'm going to grab my first aid kit and call for an ambulance. Can you tell me what hurts?"

He shook his head once before groaning again. "Call my club."

"Your what?" It was then I noticed the leather vest he wore and the tell-tale one percent patch on the front of it. "You want me to call your club?" I asked as I pointed at the patch.

"They won't harm you. Need them to get my bike." His voice was trailing off.

"I don't know how to call them."

He quickly rattled off a number that I put in my phone on instinct. My fingers pushed to dial before I realized what I was doing. "Shit, I really need to call for help."

"Club first."

I rolled my eyes just as someone picked up. "Baffle," the gravelly voice spat out.

"A man just crashed in front of me on US-60 headed into New Mexico from Arizona. He's one of yours." As I rattled off the information something glinted from across the street. My eyes tracked the source. There was a man crouched down behind some scrub on the other side of the road. If he'd been there the whole time, it was a small miracle the accident hadn't been worse.

He wasn't watching me. The man's eyes were trained on the fallen biker. It only took another second for me to process the fact that the glint I'd seen a moment ago was from the rifle in his hands. My headlights created enough light that his scope picked it up and reflected it back.

Without another thought, I dropped my cell phone and snatched my sidearm out of my holster, aimed, released my breath, and pulled the trigger. I wasn't stupid. If he planned to shoot the biker on the side of the road, there was no way he would leave me behind as a witness to what happened.

3

I heard a harsh voice yelling in the background and realized the noise came from the cell I dropped.

"Who the fuck is this and what is going on?" I could hear him giving orders to someone in the background as I glanced down and snatched the phone back up while keeping my Springfield 10 mil trained on the man who I'd just shot.

"Your man, I think he's passed out now," I called into the phone as I took a quick glance down at the biker again. "His vest thing says 'President' on it. Wait..." I glanced around and realized the tape under it probably showed his name. After I dusted it off, I called out his road name. "Bigfoot."

"Prez is down. We gotta go!" the man yelled into the phone before he started to speak to me again. "How bad is it?"

"He was more worried about his motorcycle getting picked up, it's a few feet away from where he landed. We have a bigger problem, though."

"Does that bigger problem have to do with the gunshot I just heard?"

"There was a man on the other side of the road. He was just about to take a shot at your president when I took him out. Your brother needs an ambulance in a bad way, but there's a body here that I'm responsible for now as well."

"You shot the man? Are you sure he's dead?"

"Well, I'm no expert, but I am a good shot, and he hasn't moved since."

"Listen, darlin', we're bringing a doc with us. Do not call anyone."

"I can't make any guarantees that someone else won't call or that the truck driver whose blown tire took out your president won't make his way back." A thought occurred to me then. "Shit! What if the guy I shot was working with the truck driver? He seemed pretty hell-bent on passing me and the motorcycle." I hoped like hell that wasn't the case and continued to ramble my fears away.

"If it was a civilian, they might have called the cops about getting their tire shot out, if they realized that was what happened. Then again, why wouldn't a trucker pull over to fix his tire, even if he didn't realize he took a man out with the one that blew?" I was rambling, but my brain wouldn't stop turning over as the possibilities came crashing down around me.

"Fuck, lady. Shut up! We have a guy that is two minutes out from you. Name's Jester and he's in a white work van with ladders on top."

"You're sending a murder van, and you want me to be okay with it?"

"A what?" the man on the other end of the line asked. "Never mind. Look, stay put and do what you can for Bigfoot."

I hung up the cell and stuffed it back in my pocket. Bigfoot was awake again when I glanced down to check on him. "I have to make sure the asshole across the street is dead," I explained. He seemed to understand and attempted a nod. It was such a subtle movement that I couldn't be sure. I ran across the road and checked on the asshole who had the rifle trained on the crashed biker. There was no need to check for a pulse when I got there. It was obvious he was dead since half his head was blown off. I had aimed for center mass, as I'd always been taught, but since he was crouched down, that was about as central as I could get. His head was in pieces on the ground around him.

There was no point in lingering around a corpse. I snatched his rifle up and then ran back across the highway as I sent up a silent prayer and thanked my lucky stars that no one else seemed to be traveling this late – or early, I supposed. Once I got back to Bigfoot, I crouched down and checked on him again. He was still breathing and didn't appear to be bleeding profusely. That didn't mean much, since it was the internal bleeding that would probably kill him after taking that kind of impact and rolling the way he did.

"I would take your helmet off, but I'm honestly afraid that it would do more harm than good." I kept any signs of panic out of my voice as I assessed the man. I was halfway down his body, palpating for possible damage when a dingy, white work van with ladders on top pulled off near where Bigfoot's motorcycle came to rest.

"What's going on, Bigfoot? Are you taking a nap on the side of the road?" the man joked, but I could tell by the way his eyes tracked every inch of his friend that he was just trying to put the man at ease. The newcomer was worried, and that quickly turned to fear when he realized his buddy didn't answer back.

"He's been fading in and out, but there isn't a lot of blood." Bigfoot groaned as though he were in a lot of pain. "On the outside, anyway," I tacked on. "There is a body over there, and I would appreciate it if you could hide that fact before the law rolls up here and wants to know why I shot him."

The newcomer, Jester, nodded his head, hopped into his van, and positioned it across the street where he could easily load the body into the back. He took a jug of something out of his van and doused the area with it after he moved the body. When he was done with that, he pulled back over and started to load up the motorcycle. All the while, I noticed he was having a conversation via whatever hands-free device he had clamped to his ear.

"VP wants to know how bad he is," Jester called out to me.

"Well, an eighteen-wheeler was in the middle of passing us on the left when his tire blew, and a huge chunk flew into your buddy. He took the hit directly to his left side, maybe a bit of his chest too. That sent him flying over to the right side of the road while his bike took off without him and crashed where you just picked it up. He was talking to me at first and told me to call you guys before he passed out. Seemed to have a great deal of pain while trying to shake his head, so either the tire hit his neck too or the fall did enough damage that it hurt like hell. He's still breathing. I think his arm is broken. Honestly, I'm more concerned about possible internal bleeding or the damage he might have done to his head and neck. Thank fuck he wore a helmet, but I don't want to be the one to remove it."

"It's okay. Can you stick with him while I finish up here?"

"Of course."

"Did the trucker stop at all?"

"No, but I have a dash cam in my car, and it has been running the whole time."

"Do not tell the cops. If anyone happens to show up before my club, keep quiet. My VP will want that footage."

"I have reason to not want that video going to the cops, too."

"You on the lamb or something?" the man joked.

"No, I'm not on the lamb." I rolled my eyes, then rethought that. "I might be if they look at the video and see that I shot someone."

"Wait, you're the one that shot that fucker?"

"That's what I said before. He was about to kill your friend, and it didn't take a genius to determine I'd be next."

I had a healthier fear of a one percent motorcycle club than the cops, so his wish was my command at that point. It took another minute before I realized Jester was no longer focused on me. He was back across the street policing brass. He picked up one bullet casing and pocketed it. I guessed that meant he had most likely shot the truck's tire after all.

I glanced down and groaned. Hopefully, they really did have a doctor on the way, because Bigfoot didn't look too good.

I sat with the man, who was objectively very good looking, despite the bruises and swelling that started to bloom all over his face. His leathers were toast, and his helmet was scuffed and dented in spots. It appeared it might also be cracked on the side, but I didn't want to speculate what that might mean for his head.

"Do I take your helmet off or leave it?" I wondered out loud. "What if your head swells and..."

"Off," the man groaned.

I jumped. "Oh shit, I thought you were still passed out."

He huffed at me as if to say he was until I bothered him with my inane questions. I carefully reached up and unlatched his chin strap and then put one hand under the base of his neck and head to support it while I gently removed his helmet.

"Okay, Bigfoot, I'm just going to put my sweater underneath your head, so it isn't resting on the ground." The sweater had been tied around my waist because it was too hot to wear earlier when I was in a crowd of people. Then I got chilly after getting into my truck. The heater took forever to kick in and push out anything but cold air. Since I had been sitting on my sweater at that point, I put on my emergency jacket I always kept in my truck – for when the stupid, temperamental heater refused to blow hot.

"Mmm," The sound – something between an appreciative moan and a painful groan – was all he managed. It was then that my eyes drifted down his body, assessing for further damage again.

"Yep, you definitely broke that arm," I said aloud, even though it appeared he had passed out again. I saw blood near the waistband of his jeans and gently pulled his shirt up to have a look. It didn't appear as though there were any deep gouges or anything. It was more like he had really bad road rash. His jeans on his left side were worn down in spots and there was a bit of blood seeping through there as well. Thankfully, nothing I could see looked life-threatening. If the man didn't have internal bleeding and his head didn't swell up and pop off, then he might be okay after all. His left arm drooped at a weird angle making me think it had either been dislocated or something worse. Considering there wasn't any blood coming from up there, I hoped it meant everything was still attached.

"I guess this would be a good time for me to be a nurse or a doctor or know more than basic first aid," I murmured to myself and was surprised when the man attempted to chuckle. "Oh God, I'm sorry. I didn't mean to make you laugh."

"No apologies," he insisted in a garbled way that was barely understandable.

"Your men are on the way." It was the only reassurance I could give him as we waited in the dark along the lonely stretch of highway in the middle of the night. I shivered and realized the temperatures had dropped again. I took my jacket off and draped it across his torso. There was a chance he couldn't even feel the difference, but it was the only thing I knew to do that might not harm him more.

We sat on the roadside for another ten minutes as Jester did his thing cleaning up the mess on the other side of the road. It looked as though he was policing for more brass over there and combing through the brush. It made sense. Beyond the tire being blown out, it might tell us something more if he were to find other casings, or perhaps evidence that the man had been lying in wait for a long time. I didn't believe in coincidences, so the probability of a man lying in wait with a rifle at the exact place an eighteen-wheeler's tire blew to take out a motorcycle, felt a little too convenient to be anything else but an ambush.

I heard the distant roar of motorcycles. "Doc is coming with the men; he'll be able to assess things. If we need to run him to the hospital, we'll take him ourselves." I glanced up to see Jester was back, and he stared down at me with a strange look in his eyes.

"Not sure that's smart. What if moving him makes things worse or delaying treatment gets him dead?" I asked

"M'k," Bigfoot huffed. I was fairly certain it was his way of saying he was okay enough to wait, but I didn't believe him for a minute, especially since he passed out again after mumbling almost incoherently.

"Jester!"

"Yeah?"

"If he dies on me, I'm going to kill the person who made him wait for treatment."

The man chuckled and came to stand beside me. "Bigfoot's a tough bastard. He'll pull through."

"Says you."

"Yep, I've seen enough riders go down in my time that I can tell you with certainty that he'll have one hell of a recovery, but he'll live."

"I hope so."

"Also, it ain't wise to threaten to off our VP, since he's the one who gave the order."

"Whatever, I'm not scared of him."

"I guess you wouldn't be, considering I just cleaned up the last body you dropped."

"That was also the first," I admitted.

"Well, you did a good job of it, lady." He glanced across the road and then back at me. "You were standing over here?"

"Yeah?"

"You used that?" He pointed at the 10 mil that was secured into my holster. I nodded. "Big sidearm for a little lady."

"Not really. They fire smoothly, barely any kickback."

Jester nodded his head. "Fifty feet give or take to where the fucker was lying in wait." When I didn't say anything, he tacked on, "In the dark and high on adrenaline." He was assessing my skill level, I realized. "You a cop?"

I laughed at his question. "Not by a long shot."

"Former military?"

I gave a quick nod. "No combat duty, but served honorably, nonetheless. The military doesn't account for my shooting skills, though. That would be my Uncle Brady's doin'."

"Why did good ol' Uncle Brady decide to teach his precious niece how to shoot so well?"

"Because he wanted me to be able to defend myself if it was ever necessary."

I glanced down to see that Bigfoot's eyes were open again. "Took a little nap again, huh?" I asked as the distant rumble of motorcycle engines grew heavier in the air. The ground seemed to vibrate as they moved closer, too. "Your friends are almost here."

I felt a squeeze on my hand and glanced down to see that Bigfoot managed to get his good hand over to mine. "Thank you."

"Don't mention it. Saved me from a boring night of going home to wash my hair."

"What the fuck?" Jester asked as he laughed and looked down at his phone – presumably to see the time.

I shrugged my shoulders. "That was my excuse when I left the double date from hell. My coworker Jake convinced me to go to this concert over in Arizona with his girlfriend and another guy. Basically, he set me up to be the fourth wheel to a threesome he didn't know he was involved in."

"Let me guess, the set-up date was more interested in you than your buddy's girl and it pissed her off?"

I nodded my agreement. "Exactly that. When Matt seemed too interested, Sandra lost it and started screaming at him that the date wasn't meant to be real." I started to mimic her tone. "How dare you act like you're interested in someone else – in front of me!" I shook my head and remembered Jake had seemed upset by the revelation, but not entirely shocked. It made me wonder if he had asked me so that he could get exactly that response from his girlfriend. I don't like to feel used by people. Jake and I would have it out about that shit later. He should have found a better way to bust his cheating girlfriend, like hire a PI or something. That's what normal people did.

Jester laughed and Bigfoot squeezed my hand again. I could have sworn he smiled, but then again, most of his face was a swollen mess already, so it could have been a twitch of pain.

"Sorry," I apologized on a whisper. "I forgot I'm not supposed to make you laugh. You probably have a broken rib or three. Know for a fact that stuff hurts." I glanced back up at Jester to finish my story. "So, when the crap hit the fan, I said I had to go home and wash my hair."

"Left your boy there to deal with the fallout of a cheating girlfriend?"

I groaned. "He put me in that situation knowing full well I've always thought she was a giant freaking diseased twat."

"You don't have a filter, do you?" the man inquired.

"Nah. I don't really see the point. If people don't like what I have to say, they can pretty much fuck off."

"If he don't claim you after he wakes the fuck up, I'm next in line," Jester said and then jogged back to his van as the first motorcycle rolled up.

I tilted my head to the side and chuckled. "What do ya know? It really is a murder van."

"Fuck's sake," Bigfoot mumbled as his chest shook.

"Sorry," I whispered again.

2. BAFFLED

SAMMY

Just as one of the motorcycles pulled up next to us, I glanced down to see that Bigfoot was out of it again. The new arrival hopped off his motorcycle and headed directly to us. He assessed his friend as if he had training as a battlefield medic. Maybe he did.

"Jester took care of the body?" he asked and immediately I recognized his voice. My eyes drifted down to where his road name was written and sure enough, he was Baffle, the club's vice president. The same man I spoke with on the phone.

"Yes, he got everything packed away in his murder van." I quirked up an eyebrow at him because it was apparently an apt description.

"Don't think you can complain about that, since it was your murder we cleaned up with the van."

I shrugged my shoulders. "Not murder if it's self-defense."

"True enough. How long has he been out?"

"He comes and goes. I think the pain is the cause, more

so than any potential head wound. His helmet seems to have done a good job." Baffle picked up the helmet in question and winced when he noticed the crack down the side.

"Did you take this off?"

"He asked me to. Plus, I thought it might be important for your doc to be able to see his head, assess for swelling, bleeding, or whatever else."

Baffle nodded at me just as Jester walked up again. "Handed keys off to the prospect. He took the van back to the clubhouse for us."

"Good," Baffle replied. His dark eyes seemed almost black in the limited light, since his back was to my headlights. His dark hair blended with the night and the leather of his cut. It almost gave him a grim reaper appeal, except that was an unsettling thought considering I didn't want the man I'd tended to in all of this to lose the battle for his life.

"She tell you about the dash cam yet?" Jester asked.

Baffle shook his head and then brought his eyes up to meet mine for the first time. Yep, they looked black even in the light. "So, I have a dash cam on my truck that recorded the whole thing. She's probably still recording, since I didn't think to turn it off."

"Grab that cam!" Baffle ordered. "I want whatever backup file it goes to."

"It operates off a large flash drive. When it runs out of space, it alerts me, and I can either record over what I already have or stop it there and feed it a new memory stick."

"Why do you have it?" Baffle asked.

"Are you kidding? I hit a fucking elk a few years back and insurance tried to tell me I could have avoided the bastard. After having to fight with them to pay out the damages, I swore I'd never be without proof again." I glanced back at my beat-to-hell, powder blue Toyota. "They shorted me so much that I wasn't able to replace my old 2500-series. That's all I could afford when all was said and done, and even that wasn't cheap since it's a Toyota."

"Fair enough." The man turned to another MC member. "Grunt, grab that memory stick."

"Wait a minute!" I called out. "No offense, but I don't know or trust you guys. There is clear evidence of me shooting a firearm at something across the road."

Baffle stood to his full, beyond six-foot height and stared down at me menacingly, as if that would have some sort of effect on me. "It won't show the person you shot, so it doesn't matter."

"It will show us standing here talking about it," I sassed back.

Baffle rolled his eyes. "Look, the club already owes you for taking care of our Prez, what more do you want?"

I glanced around as they all waited for me to answer. "I want to stay with him until he wakes back up."

"Why?"

"Why?" I asked before I narrowed my eyes on him. "Why would I want to make sure the man I saw thrown from his motorcycle, and who I killed someone for, wakes up? Gee, I don't know, maybe because I need to know he's going to be okay."

Baffle nodded and then tipped his head toward my truck. "Follow behind us, then. I promise you can stay with him as long as it takes to appease your big heart. If he wakes up and wants you gone-"

"Then I'm gone," I stated quickly.

I was destined to be in Arizona, apparently. That was where we headed instead of where I knew the MC's clubhouse to be. The minute I realized we were headed back in the direction I'd come from earlier, I almost decided that it didn't matter what happened to the man. Nothing good had come out of my little trip across the state line before, and I didn't think that would change as I crossed into Arizona again. It took a few minutes for me to realize that we were headed toward the White Mountain Emergency Room. I breathed out a sigh of relief that they were going to take their buddy to an actual hospital to get him treated. I didn't want to imagine what would happen if they tried to treat his injuries themselves.

When we got there, I parked as close as I could to the door without being in the way of all the men who had caught up and followed us there on their motorcycles. I was out of my truck and headed inside before most of them had even managed to back into their spots. Baffle was already there, along with a man who barked orders at the medical staff.

"Dr. Waters," One of the nurses nodded her head toward the man who wore the same motorcycle club cut that the other men wore. I guess when they said they had a doc on the way, they hadn't lied.

"We need to get him into an MRI, Mercedes."

"Yes, sir." The nurse and some other staff wheeled Bigfoot off behind a set of doors as Dr. Waters turned to speak in rushed, hushed tones with Baffle. I stood there, not knowing what to do with myself until Jester came in and pulled me aside.

"Come on, sweetheart, let's settle in over here for a minute until they know more."

I followed along, not that I had much choice, since his arm was wrapped around my shoulders as the biker who cleaned up after my mess earlier guided us toward some chairs in the corner of the waiting room. His warmth seeped into me, and it was only then that I realized I had no clue what happened to my sweater or the jacket I used to cover Bigfoot. Not that it mattered, except the air condition in the hospital was cranked to full-blast despite it being a chilly night. I shivered involuntarily and Jester pulled me closer.

"You cold or is the adrenaline starting to crash?" he asked. I leaned my head back to look up into a pair of deep brown eyes that seemed legitimately worried about me. I managed to shrug my shoulders before another shiver ran through me. "Prospect!" Jester called out in a tone that said someone better answer him immediately.

"What's up, Jester?" A boy answered. There was no other way to describe him, as he was so thin, and looked incredibly young.

"Run out and grab a hoodie from the van." Jester threw the kid a set of keys and then sat me down in a chair next to him. All the while, his arm remained around my shoulders.

We sat there for a few minutes as the rest of the club brothers filtered into the waiting room and took seats surrounding us. There was a wall directly next to Jester, since he'd seated us in the corner, but the seats in front and beside us were filled with motorcycle men, which put a buffer at least three men deep in either direction between me and the next non-motorcycle club brother in the waiting room.

Baffle finally made his way to us, but I didn't like the angry look on his face as he did. When he got to us, he squatted down in front of me and looked me straight in the eye. Yup, his eyes were still so dark brown they appeared black, even under the shitty fluorescent lights of the hospital.

"Someone called it in. I can only assume the trucker did after his buddy didn't catch up to him." That was disturbing information.

"He was behind me for a good haul," I muttered. There was no need to say the rest out loud. Whoever Bigfoot's enemies were, they might know exactly who I was and that I stopped to help him. The disappearance of the shooter would be linked to me.

"I know. We're handling it. These men," Baffle stated as he tipped his head to indicate the human wall of his club brothers that surrounded me, "are here to protect you until we can get Prez in a room and you in there with him. Then we'll make sure no one gets to either of you while you're both here."

I gave a sharp nod of my head, but then I groaned. "You said someone called it in. They called the police?"

"Quickest way for them to assess what happened to their hitman."

"They have to work out logistics, since we crossed state lines to get Bigfoot to the hospital. Rest assured someone will come and they will want to speak to you."

"What do you want me to say to them?" I asked.

Baffle and Jester shared a look that said they were shocked that I would cooperate that easily. "You don't mind leaving pieces of the details out?" Baffle questioned.

"Not at all. As far as I'm concerned, a truck blew a tire and kept going. Your friend was thrown from his bike, and I stopped to help him until you got there. Nothing else to say." I gave him a solid look. "I assume you've already taken any evidence that I had a dash cam up?" I whispered my question, as if someone might overhear me. It wasn't necessary, but it made me feel better.

"We have it," Baffle assured me as the prospect made his way back to us.

The boy extended his arm out over the shoulders of the row of men who sat immediately in front of me. "Thanks," I continued to whisper as I took the hoodie. My hands shook as I tried to pull the bottom open, so Jester took his arm from around me and helped me pull the hoodie over my head and settle it around my body. When my head popped back through the hole, I noticed Baffle gave him a weird look. Jester gave a quick shake of his head, as if in answer to a question that hadn't been asked.

"I used my sweater and jacket for your president, but I don't know what happened to them," I explained. It felt like that might have been what Baffle wanted to know. It was clear the sweatshirt I had been given belonged to a club member, since it had the masked skull king logo on it that the club used to identify themselves.

"We'll get you replacements," Baffle insisted as he patted my leg and then stood in front of me. He turned to some of the men who had been silently watching our interaction. "No one gets to her. Prez wants her kept safe."

That was news to me. I wondered when that had been determined. Then again, Baffle had ridden with him to the hospital, so I had to assume they spoke on the way.

"What about LEO?" one of them asked him.

"Especially LEO. We'll make sure she has someone with her at all times." I guess he didn't trust me to keep my word about not mentioning the shooter.

"I meant what I said."

Baffle glanced down at me. "Don't know you, why you were really there tonight, or what the fuck you have going on, lady. Someone will be by your side until I say otherwise." His commanding tone said that he wouldn't put up with any arguments from me. "Going to check and see how shit's going. Keep her by your side and nothing more." Baffle gave Jester another weird look that I couldn't decipher, but the man didn't say a single word back to his vice president. Instead, he tapped his hand on my knee twice and then sat back and spread his legs out, as if he was the most relaxed man on the planet. As if he hadn't cleaned up a murder, helped his injured friend, and looked out for me. I'd think their behavior was weird had I not done my time in the Army. Their ability to speak full conversations with just looks was reminiscent of some of the people I'd worked beside over the years.

3. AN ANGEL AMONG US
BIGFOOT

"Ma'am, we really need your statement," I heard some asshole practically growl. Fuck, my head was more than a little fuzzy, but I knew exactly where I was. A motherfuckin' hospital.

"I already told you." A woman, who sounded vaguely familiar, snapped at him. "Open your damn ears and listen to the words that already came out of my mouth. I was driving on US-60 in the dark. There was a motorcycle in front of me. One minute all was well. The next, he was flying through the air. I must have looked down, or maybe I forgot because shock set in as I was trying to keep him alive on the side of the road, but I don't even remember seeing what caused his accident. I can't say it in any other way. I can't make it any plainer for you. That is all I know."

"Yeah, sure. You're trying to convince us this man is a total stranger to you. You happened to be behind him on the road when he wrecked, you called his club instead of 9-1-1, and now you conveniently don't know what happened. And here you are sitting vigil by his bedside waiting for the man to wake up."

"Obviously, you've never trauma-bonded with someone. I held this man's bloody head in my hands. I waited with him as he came to and passed out several times on the side of the road. Should I have left him there to be hit by someone else?"

"You should have called us first." The man – who I figured was a cop – told her.

"Well, the only thing he said to me was 'Call my brothers,' and so I did. He was worried about his motorcycle."

I opened my eyes in time to catch the officer roll his at the woman. I dragged my eyes toward her and immediately sucked in an audible breath. My guardian angel was just as gorgeous as I thought she was. "You," I managed to say.

"Hey!" She spun around and grabbed hold of my hand again. "I was so worried about you. Do you remember me?"

I tried to nod, but it hurt, so I stopped.

"You should stay still. The doctor mentioned you have a pretty nasty concussion which probably isn't being helped by this guy yammering on and being as loud as is humanly possible without purposefully yelling." She made the declaration sound like she was scolding a child. I wanted to laugh but was afraid it would hurt.

"Name?" I questioned.

"Oh, I guess we missed out on real introductions earlier. I'm Samantha Morton, but pretty much everyone calls me Sam or Sammy."

"Sammy." The attempt to say her name was more whisper than word. "My angel," I managed to say before being pulled back under into the darkness.

4. RESCUE

SAMMY

"My angel," Bigfoot called me just before he passed out again.

"Since he didn't know her name, kinda sounds like she might be telling the truth," the nicer of the two police officers said.

Officer Not-So-Friendly huffed at me in frustration. "If we find out a crime was committed and you withheld information from us, you will be charged as an accessory."

"Are you seriously threatening me right now?"

"If no crimes were committed, it wouldn't feel like a threat," the bastard argued back.

"No, it felt like a threat because you meant for it to be exactly that. You can leave now because I have nothing further to say to you. One minute I was coming back from a concert double-date from hell and the next I looked up and that guy's motorcycle was flying through the air one way while he fell and rolled the other. That is all I will ever know. And let's be clear, even if I knew something else, you would be the last person I'd trust at this point. Thanks for making me have so much faith in the system." I turned my back on him and muttered, "Asshole," under my breath.

"Sounds like the lady wants you to get the fuck out. Pretty sure the doctor told you not to be in here disturbing her patient anyway," the man I had come to know as Baffle, the Vice President of the Kings of Anarchy MC New Mexico Chapter said as he strolled into the room.

"Watch yourself," Officer Dipshit growled threateningly.

"Boy, you better get out of here before the lady notices you pissed yourself trying to talk to me like that."

The officer bucked up, but his partner grabbed ahold of him and maneuvered the asshole out the door.

"How long were you there?" I asked Baffle once they were gone.

"Long enough to know you didn't give them shit, so no worries."

I waved his answer away. "That wasn't even a worry of mine. Your president woke up for a minute and he seemed to know who I was, so hopefully there's no issues with the impact his head took."

"That's really good to know. Thanks, darlin." Baffle pulled the second chair closer, so that we were seated side-by-side. We both sat, staring at his club brother and lost in our own thoughts. Time passing wasn't really something I registered until he spoke again. My back ached with the effort to sit in an unforgiving chair for so long. "He's woken once already. You don't have to stay."

"Is that your way of trying to get rid of me?" I asked and turned so I could see what Baffle's response would be.

He shook his head. "Not at all. Honestly, I'm trying to let you off the hook here. Not sure why you feel obligated to hang around, but he has people who will look out for him."

I gave a quick nod of my head. "Have you ever seen someone crash like that?" The slightest tip of his head in acknowledgment was my only answer. "Well, I haven't. I can't find the words to explain why I'm still sitting here with a stranger. He needed me on the side of that road because the asshole who hit him didn't stop." I lowered my voice to a whisper. "There were also the other threats and no one else was there. Maybe it's a weird way to look at things, but I feel like I need to see it through and let him know that he was never alone. I guess, if the roles were reversed, it would be nice to know I wasn't left alone in my moment of weakness for someone to maybe come take advantage of."

"If you have skeletons in your closet that put you in that mindset, you let me know and we will settle up for you. After the loyalty you showed our president and the club, we owe you that much."

The smile I offered him was genuine as I spoke. "There hasn't been anything like that. It just freaks me out to know that I could be sitting in the hospital with no one looking out for me, or worse, left to die on the side of the road by myself. It doesn't make sense. I know that. Still, I'll be here until he wakes up for longer than two minutes. When I'm sure he'll be okay, I'll head out."

Baffle tipped his head again and then stared at me thoughtfully.

"That camera footage helped a lot."

"Good, I'm glad."

"It showed you in your badass stance when you took aim across the road. Protected our prez when he was not able to do it himself. Won't ever forget that. Doesn't matter that your life was on the line, too. Matters that you acted and stayed the course."

A shiver ran up my spine at the reminder of the other thing I'd done. It wasn't something I consciously thought about until it was dragged back up. "I think maybe there's something broken inside me," I mumbled without meaning to say it out loud.

"Why is that?"

I glanced up and shook my head briefly. "I keep forgetting about doing that. It's like, duh, it happened, but it doesn't even register as being important. At least, not until you just brought it up again." We were both silent for a minute before I added, "It should, though. Right? It should be at the top of the list of things that mattered about last night."

Baffle leaned forward and took one of my hands in his. "We all process shit in our own time. It might not hit you until you're back home and comfortable in your own surroundings. It might never really sink in. Sometimes shock, or the adrenaline high, trick your brain into forgetting or trivializing a situation, so you feel distanced from it. It's almost like you saw it in a movie instead of having it happen to you."

"Makes sense, I guess. That's kind of what it feels like."

"If or when it hits, you need someone to talk to about it, you have my number."

"Why?"

"Like I said, the club owes you. Least I can do is be there for you if shit gets too real in your head and you have trouble dealing."

"Thanks. I don't think I will, but I appreciate the offer anyway."

"You sure about sticking around?" Baffle looked antsy, like he wanted to be anywhere else but the hospital.

"Yeah, if you need to get going, I'll be here."

"Great. I wouldn't ask, but since you'll be here anyway, I'd rather him not wake up alone." He took two steps back toward the door. "We have club business, trying to find out why things happened the way they did that night."

I nodded. "I hope you figure it out and handle the situation accordingly." I could speak in code as well as any of the motorcycle men who had been doing just that since they rolled up to the accident scene. Baffle threw me a wicked grin and turned to head out the door.

Once he was gone, my attention returned to the man lying in the hospital bed. Even through the bruising and swelling on his face, I could tell the man was attractive. Honestly, he was probably shit hot under all that purple and blue. He had what must normally be a well-kept beard and mustache. It was full but trimmed neatly and peppered through with enough silver strands to tell me that he had a few years on me without being old enough to be my father. His hair was likewise neatly trimmed at the sides and longer on top.

I reached up and pushed some of that hair back off his forehead and took a closer look at the bruising along his hairline. Bigfoot had been lucky. If he hadn't been wearing that helmet, I don't think he would have survived. I shook that thought off before it could form images I didn't want to clog up my already fucked-up memories of that night.

My phone buzzed from my pocket and I sat back to pull it out.

Jake: Where are you?

Sammy: Hospital with a friend.

Jake: I didn't think you had any friends.

Sammy: Thanks, asshole.

Jake: Sorry, I came in with flowers to apologize for what happened, but Brady said you might not be in this week.

Sammy: Like I said, hospital with a friend.

Jake: Is this like having to leave a concert to go wash your hair or is it something real?

Sammy: Get back to work, Jake.

Jake: I really am sorry. Will you forgive me? Maybe go out on a date with me sometime, now that I'm not seeing Sandra anymore?

Sammy. Forgiven and no thanks.

Jake: That was cold.

Sammy: We don't like each other like that. Don't make it a thing.

Jake: Fine. See you when you get back from the "hospital with a friend".

I chuckled over the fact that he thought I was blowing smoke up his ass. Jake wasn't someone I would ever date. As my eyes lifted to the man in the hospital bed, I knew why. Jake was soft. Granted, he had a decent body and was capable enough as a mechanic, but he wasn't someone I could see myself with. There was something about him that I knew I'd have to take care of him all the time and not the other way around. I'd bet money that if Bigfoot wasn't lying there recovering from his accident, he would be a force that couldn't be ignored. He had to be, since he was President of the local Kings of Anarchy MC. His job description alone said he was capable of taking care of whoever belonged to him. Whether it was his club brothers or whatever woman was one day lucky enough to call him hers.

No, Jake didn't stack up to Bigfoot even while the man was unconscious. I chuckled again as their differences became painfully obvious. Jake's muscles certainly didn't have anything on this man, and if I were being really honest with myself, that silver interspersed with his brown hair was sexier than I cared to admit. I shouldn't feel that way. Lord knows, he might not have been old enough to be my dad, but he was certainly old enough to be my dad's younger brother. Brady had to be close to his age.

Speaking of, my Uncle Brady would probably kick my ass all the way back to Violence if he knew who my "friend" was. He didn't have anything against the Kings, but he'd always warned me to keep my distance from them, too. It had never been a problem since I worked on the campground side of my family's business and moonlighted in the big garage when people needed repairs on their RVs. The motorcycle shop was across the property, and I never ventured there. It was the only place I really would have come into contact with the MC's members. They didn't have a shop of their own, so my uncle would sometimes lend out a bay in his shop to their club's mechanic to do routine maintenance on their motorcycles. Any major repairs, Uncle Brady did himself.

My attention shifted back to the man in front of me. I leaned over and took his hand in mine. He never woke up, but I felt him squeeze my hand just the same. I hoped he woke up sooner rather than later, because I needed to get back to my life - even if it was sort of a lonely and mostly reclusive existence on my family's compound.

5. WAKING MOMENTS
BIGFOOT

Everything was quiet when I woke, and the lights were all turned down low. It must have been late. When I turned my head as far as I could before white-hot pain shot up my neck to the base of my brain, I saw her there - the woman who stopped to help me. She was slumped in an uncomfortable-looking chair. Her hair had been thrown up on top of her head in some messy up-do that looked like it would wobble all over the place if she moved in the slightest. A couple reddish-brown tendrils escaped the knot, and one fell across the bridge of her nose. Either the lighting played tricks on my eyes, or she had freckles dotting her nose and cheeks. It wasn't something I remembered from before, but she could have been wearing makeup, or I might have been in too much pain to see the details.

I wanted to see her eyes. I needed to know if they were really as mesmerizing as I thought or if I'd been imagining shit. The way she was slumped to the side and curled up into a ball on that chair, I didn't have high hopes for her feeling great when she woke up. I glanced around to see if anyone else was in the room because I wanted to know why my brothers hadn't been looking out for her. She should have been given a pullout bed or something. As I scanned the room, my eyes met with my best friend's.

"Hey, man. Sammy told me you woke up for a few minutes earlier."

"I did?" I questioned, then wondered who the hell Sammy was. "Sammy?"

Baffle flicked his eyes to the woman in the chair. "Do you remember her?"

"She was there, but I didn't know her name."

"You don't remember waking up before?" My VP asked.

"No."

"She wouldn't leave," he informed me as I continued to stare at the woman. She was beautiful in that girl-next-door way I never really found attractive before. Obviously, she was beautiful, but if we had met under any other circumstances, I might not have given her a second glance. I would have written her off as a civilian who would never fit into my world. She wore jeans that were a little dirty-maybe stained-at the knees and a club sweatshirt that swamped her frame.

"Whose shirt?"

Baffle laughed, though he made sure to do it quietly. "Jester. You might have some competition there."

"Fucker has an ol' lady."

"We both know she hasn't been around in more than a year."

I turned my attention back to my club brother. "Fuck that."

Baffle laughed again and then shook his head at me. "Fucking hell, you're both smitten with the little crack shot."

"Crack shot?" That was confusing. What in the hell had she done to earn that nickname? Baffle got up, picked his chair up, and moved it as close to my bed as he could get, on the opposite side from where Sammy remained asleep.

"Do you remember anything about the accident?"

"Her. I remember her."

"Do you remember anything besides the girl?"

I shook my head, and my VP sat back for a minute and assessed me. "An eighteen-wheeler passed both of you, Sammy was behind you. One of the truck's tires blew and took you and your bike out. From what we gathered after seeing the dash cam video from Sammy's truck and what she had to say, that tire didn't blow. It was shot out."

"Who the fuck was shooting?"

"Mojave Devils MC. According to his cut, he was their Road Captain."

"Who the fuck are the Mojave Devils?"

"They have settled here in eastern Arizona, a little too close to the New Mexico border for my taste." Baffle glanced up at Sammy again before he turned his attention back to me. "She doesn't know it was another club yet. From what we've gathered, they're working with Rivera Cartel and looking for a better way to get shipments through from Mexico."

"Shipments of what?"

"Don't know yet," he answered.

"Fuck." I glanced over at Sammy again. Her chest still rose and fell steadily. She was down for the count, but what would they do when she woke up? "The shooter?" I finally remembered that someone had to have been there with us if a tire was shot out.

"Our girl here was packing, and she took him out just before he could pop another shot off at you."

"Son of a..." My eyes darted from Baffle to Sammy. "She needs to be protected. Saved my life," I got out before a dry patch in the back of my throat made me cough. The cough pulled at my sore ribs and sent pain lancing through my chest. "Motherfucker!" I hissed.

"I'll get the nurse to get you some more pain meds." Baffle stood, but I reached out and stopped him.

"No, wait. Don't want that shit to take me down again. Water," I demanded. He moved around to get me some water which I sucked back slowly. I didn't trust my stomach to hold anything. After I finally quenched my thirst and Baffle set my cup back on the little table that was rolled off to the side, I made sure to get his full attention. "She saved me."

"She did."

"Called you, not the cops." Baffle nodded in agreement. "Shot that fucker before he killed me." Again, he simply nodded and waited to see where I was going with everything.

"She also didn't tell the cops anything when they were here."

"She's mine," I informed my VP. "Claiming her."

His soft laugh made me turn back his way. "Serious. She's mine."

"She refused to leave your side until you are fully awake, so as long as you don't wake up, I guess she's yours too."

"Fucker."

"Seriously, you should have a conversation with her when she wakes. Let her know where your head is and that she has our protection. I've already told her as much, but I don't think she understands what it means. Pretty sure she's planning to haul ass out of here as soon as she's sure you're going to be okay."

"No. She has to stay."

"Okay, well, Melissa is bringing Hawk by tomorrow to see you, so you should probably find the time to explain who they are before they get here."

"You couldn't get Hawk and bring him here without her?" I asked, knowing that if Melissa showed up, she would cause a big scene somehow. She wasn't the worst woman I could have knocked up over the years. Lis took care of our son really well, but she could be high maintenance and territorial when she thought another woman was getting too close to me. It wasn't that she was deluded enough to think we would ever be a couple, but I think she couldn't imagine what it would be like if another woman stepped in and made a family with her son's father. She didn't want to be the odd woman on the outside of a family unit looking in.

"You know Melissa. She refused to allow it. Said if her son had to visit you in the hospital, he would have his mom there." Baffle rolled his eyes. "She's going to coddle Hawk right into being a little pussy momma's boy."

"That's my son you're talking about."

"I know that, fucker. Warning you about what's gonna happen if you don't put your foot down with his mom about shit."

"What if she gets spooked by Lis and Hawk?" I asked, knowing my club brother would give it to me straight.

"She's still here when she could have walked away. Killed a man to save your life."

"Probably to save her own skin, not that I blame her for that."

"Still, she's crashed out in your hospital room. Refuses to leave. Prospect had to bring her some food earlier. Same clothes she's had on since we got to the hospital."

"How'd she end up in Jester's hoodie?"

"She gave you her sweater and her jacket. Both were ruined, poor thing was shaking and shivering in the waiting room while they took you for an MRI. Sent the prospect to go grab something out of the cage we brought you here in. Cage is Jester's territory, since he keeps the vans running for club business."

"Tell him she's mine." I growled. My eyes drooped as warmth flushed through my body.

"Looks like meds kicked back in. Sleep tight, brother." Baffle sounded like he was a hundred miles away and then there was nothing but fucking peace and quiet.

6. INTRUDING
SAMMY

No way.

No freaking way was I sitting there having dirty fantasies about an incapacitated man only to have his woman and son show up. A woman and son no one bothered to tell me about.

Why hadn't Baffle warned me that Bigfoot had a family or that they would be stopping by the hospital?

Probably because he didn't think I was an idiot who sat by his friend's bedside having vivid daydreams about what it would be like to be with the man who was currently laid up in a hospital bed. Granted, I don't think too many people would blame me, and they'd probably do the same if they found themselves in my shoes. Still...

"Dad!" A little boy called as he ran over to Bigfoot's bedside. I stood up as quietly as possible from the unforgiving chair I'd been seated in for far too long. Unfortunately, thanks to the involuntary groan I produced when my sore muscles protested the movement, the boy realized I was there.

"Who are you?" he asked as he snapped his head around to give me his full attention. The child was kindergarten-aged replica of his father, and the narrow-eyed gaze that he turned on me held just as much suspicion as his father's might have if he were awake to wonder why in the hell I had camped out at his bedside.

"I'm nobody," I mumbled as my feet continued to shuffle back toward the door while I kept Bigfoot's family in my sight.

"Why were you with my dad? I don't know you." The boy sounded even more suspicious as his eyes tracked every tiny movement I made toward the door. I didn't miss the fact that there was a tinge of fear in his eyes too.

Great, I could add 'scares kids' to my resume.

"Boooy!" Bigfoot's voice drew the word out as he called his son's attention back to him. The sound was a rougher, grittier version of the voice I remembered from the side of the road after his crash.

"Sorry," I mumbled again as I turned to leave.

"No!" Bigfoot called out just a tad too late because I was already out the door and pretended not to hear him. I heard though. I also didn't miss the woman when she said, "I'll try to catch her."

Catch me she did, though I had serious doubts she would tell him that.

"I know who you are," the woman explained as she stepped into the hallway with me. "You're just an opportunistic bitch who was in the right place at the right time and thought she would take advantage of the situation while the Kings of Anarchy's President wasn't able to keep his guard up.

"That's why his family is here to protect him. Our son doesn't need to see some next-level club whore leech trying to take advantage of his daddy. As Bigfoot's ol' lady, you better believe I won't let it happen either."

Right. What was I supposed to say to that?

I might not have had experience with motorcycle clubs before the incident, but I'd seen enough TV to know exactly what an ol' lady was. There was nothing I could say to her, so I turned down the hallway that would lead me back to the emergency department and didn't bother to look back. I'd been in Springerville too long anyway. It was time to get back to my life in Violence. As if to remind me of that life, my phone pinged with an incoming text.

> Uncle Brady: You sure you're okay? I'm worried and so is your dad.

> Sammy: Be back to work tomorrow.

> Uncle Brady: You know that's not what I'm worried about.

> Sammy: I know. I'll explain when I get back. I'm good. Promise.

> Uncle Brady: Love you, Sammy-girl. If you're in trouble, you know you can come to me, right?

> Sammy: I know. Love you, too.

My father and his brothers weren't the overly emotional type of men who would bleed their hearts out at my feet. Uncle Brady, being the youngest of the three, was the only one who ever really told me he loved me. It wasn't that Uncle Josh or my dad didn't, they just assumed I knew and saved the words for important days - like my birthday or Christmas.

By the time I made it to the Emergency Department, I felt like the weight of the world had been dropped right on my shoulders. I knew in my heart that it was the guilt I felt. Why in the world I ever assumed a man as fine as Bigfoot was single was beyond even my own comprehension. That wasn't entirely true, though. I knew I wasn't crazy. Jester had said, "If he doesn't claim you, I will." Something to that effect anyway. Why wouldn't I think the man was free under those circumstances? Still, I was an asshole for drooling over the guy who almost died. Maybe his woman was right, and I really was an opportunistic bitch. It took this for me to realize that about myself.

"Hey, Sam! Is he awake?" I turned to see Baffle and another guy jogging to catch up to me. They both glanced around nervously like they might be expecting trouble. They shouldn't have worried. I was trouble, and I was about to take myself out of the equation.

"Sam?" Baffle questioned, and I realized I'd never answered him the first time.

"I think so."

"Did you leave him there alone?" he asked in a tone that said he was pissed at me for some reason.

My head pivoted back and forth of its own accord as I finally found the words. "His son and ol' lady showed up."

"Ol' lady?" A quick glance at the new man's cut told me his road name was Knuckles.

"Yeah, that's what she said. Look, I've got to go." I

pointed to the door that was only a few steps away as the men continued to stare at me like I might have the plague. Truthfully, I hadn't been able to brush my teeth or comb my hair with anything more than my fingers for the past couple days, so I may have looked like a plague victim.

"Glitch, get up there and check to see who is with Prez," Baffle ordered. One of the men who had caught up to Baffle and Knuckles took off immediately without even questioning the order. I guess being vice president had some perks. While he was busy tossing out orders, I made my way closer to the door. Two steps away and...

"Hey, Sam! Wait!"

Shit. I was so close. Fuck it. I didn't owe any of those men anything, least of all any more of my time. I kept going. My pace increased, and I moved as quickly in the direction of where I thought my truck was without full-on running to get there. When I didn't see my truck right away, I finally pulled my key fob out and clicked the lock. It beeped but from the opposite direction I'd been headed. Dammit!

Baffle caught up to me before I was even able to correct my course. "Sam?" he questioned. "Did you talk to Bigfoot?"

"No."

"Why not?"

"He wasn't awake until his family showed up and his son yelled out for him. I wasn't really welcome there after that."

"Did someone kick you out?"

"Not really. The little boy seemed uncomfortable with a stranger there, and his old lady mistook me for a club whore, so I..."

"A club whore?" Baffle asked as his head shot back almost as if he had been struck by the words. His gaze slid down my body and took in the sweatshirt, beat-to-hell jeans, and probably the stench that had to be emanating from my body. The sweatshirt alone did a good job of hiding any semblance of my figure, and I wasn't even going to think about what the rat's nest on top of my head looked like.

"Bigfoot doesn't-"

"Look," I cut him off. "I have to go. I stayed too long as it is, and if I don't get back to work, I won't have a job anymore." That wasn't really true since my uncle was my boss, but Baffle didn't know that. Besides, I had overstayed my welcome. Bigfoot was obviously going to make a full recovery, and his family was there to sit vigil at his bedside. He didn't need me.

"I know Bigfoot would want to speak with you, to thank you..."

"No need," I said before he could get anything else out. "Tell him I hope he heals up soon and to stay safe out there."

7. SLIPPING AWAY
BIGFOOT

"WELL, WHERE IS SHE?" I DEMANDED TO KNOW THE MINUTE Melissa walked back into my room.

"I don't know. She took off." When I continued to stare her down, Lis heaved out a put-upon sigh and rolled her eyes at me like a petulant fucking child. "She mentioned needing to get back to her life. Maybe she has a man at home waiting for her."

"She doesn't," I growled.

"How would you know?" Lis sassed back as she tugged at the ends of her blonde hair. She took the time to curl it into those big chunky waves or whatever they were before she showed up here. It hit me then that Lis was always on show whereas Sammy hadn't given a shit that she had been wearing the same clothes three days in a row. There hadn't been a bigger agenda for her than to make sure I woke up and was okay. It pissed me off that the mother of my child had taken so much time to look good before bringing my son to see me.

"Sammy was headed back to Violence after a crappy blind date when the accident happened."

"Okay, so? What's this have to do with me? Did you want me to hold her hostage or something?"

"Daddy?" I turned my glare away from Lis and softened my features before I let my eyes come to rest on Hawk.

"Hey, buddy. Sorry about that."

"Was that a nice lady?"

"The nicest," I told him.

"Nicer than my mom?"

"The lady who was here saved my life, buddy."

His eyes widened, and I immediately regretted my words as his lip poked out and his tears started to form. "You almost died?"

"I'm here, Hawk. I was in an accident and the lady got me help. Okay? I'm fine, just a little banged up."

"Can I say thank you to her for saving my daddy?"

I wish. She should have never left. Fuck. I was supposed to tell her about my boy and his mother before they ever showed up, but the damn pain meds fucked with me and kept putting me to sleep. "Maybe, if we see her again."

"Okay. Can I sit up there with you?"

"I want you to, buddy, but I'm pretty banged up and it might hurt if you accidentally bump into me."

"I don't want to hurt you."

Hawk pouted again, and I wished his mother would step in and help with this shit because my head was too fuzzy to think straight. She was too busy sulking over in the corner, though. I was about to call out to her when she turned around with tears in her eyes. "We need to figure something out, Trav. If you had died, what would I do?"

"What the hell do you mean?" Once again, it was all about her and it was really starting to piss me off.

"Daddy didn't die!" Hawk cried out to his mom.

"I'm right here, bud. Your mom's just being dramatic." I turned my attention back on Lis and gave her a look that I knew she understood, even if she tried to pretend she didn't.

"And what if?" She asked. At least she hadn't said it out loud again. "What if something happened? What am I supposed to do without you here to help with Hawk?"

"My club brothers would step up because my son will always be club family."

"Yeah? What about me, though?"

"What about you?" I argued. "You know what? We're not having this conversation in front of Hawk. It can wait until I'm out of here."

"Fine!" she snapped and turned her back on me again.

"Hey, Prez!" I turned to see Glitch standing in the door. He and his brother patched in a couple years ago, and they had quickly ingrained themselves into the heart of the New Mexico Chapter. "Baffle sent me back to check on who was here with you."

"Why?" I asked, curious as to what was so urgent that Glitch appeared to be out of breath.

"Sammy was headed out and he needed to talk to her, but she couldn't identify who was in the room with you. She said your son and ol' lady were here, but you don't have one of those," Glitched turned a very pointed, accusatory glare toward Melissa as he said that.

"What the fuck did you do?" I asked her.

"Nothing. I can't help what she assumed."

Glitch laughed. "Lying to Bigfoot?" he asked her. "She

46

told us you identified yourself as his ol' lady and that you didn't want her here."

"I never said that."

Glitch gave Melissa a look like he was ready to string her up the same way we did our enemies, and I had enough of the bullshit. "Lis, go home."

"Fine!" she snapped once again. "Come on, Hawk."

"Nope. My boy stays."

"You're in a hospital bed and can't care for him. He's coming with me."

"No!" my boy called out. "I want to stay with my dad."

"We talked about this," Lis growled at him.

"Whoa! What the fuck did you say to my son about visiting with me?" The bitch had lost her fucking mind if she thought she could coach him into not wanting to stick around and visit while I was in the hospital. I liked Lis just fine on a normal day, but that was one line she would never cross with me, or we would go to war.

"It's not like that. You can't take care of him, obviously."

"I have Glitch here," I insisted.

"And Baffle, Knuckles, Dime, and Grease are all on their way up," he added. Glitch crossed his arms over his chest, his feet shoulder-width apart, and I knew it meant he was on the defensive. He'd never liked Lis and didn't try to make nice like some of the other men in the club. Most tried to be civil for my son's sake, but we all knew she'd gotten pregnant on purpose, so there were plenty of my men who wouldn't spit on Melissa to try to save her life if she was on fire.

"As soon as you are done visiting with my son, I expect a call."

"Our son and I'll have Baffle bring him back to you when he's ready to go."

"I don't want him on a motorcycle."

"Yeah, you've made that perfectly clear, Melissa." She looked away then. My son's mother didn't like it when I called her by her full name. It usually meant I was angry with her, and she didn't like to stay on my bad side either. I refused to give her any extras when she was. Extras were things I did for her when she made my life easier instead of harder. I'd pay for spa days or shopping trips that were for her, not our son. That shit was coming to an end, though, because I was tired of the back and forth it caused.

"Where is Sammy?" I asked immediately when Baffle and Knuckles came into my hospital room.

Luckily, Melissa took off before Baffle made it back to my room. Had I known that she scared Sammy away from me, I might have done or said something I would regret in front of my boy. Only because it was done or said in front of him, though.

"She went home." My VP did not look happy to have to announce that. Knuckles bumped his arm and jerked his chin toward me. There was more, and for some reason, my club brother had been reluctant to share it with me. Dime and Grease made their way into my room and Dime immediately went to my boy.

"Hey there, little man, what do you say we go get a soda

and some candy while your dad can't do anything about it?" My boy's eyes widened like Santa had just come to dump everything he ever wanted under our tree. He looked back at me guiltily but still took Dime's hand.

"It's okay, bud. Go get a treat with Dime while my brothers keep me company. You can show me what you picked when you get back."

He pumped his little fist in the air and then took off with Dime chasing behind him. The little shit was probably afraid I would change my mind, since he wasn't allowed to have a bunch of sugary shit normally. The minute they were out of sight, my attention shifted back to Baffle. He came and sat in the chair that Sammy had been using until Melissa showed up.

"She went home and won't be back."

"What the fuck?"

"Melissa told her that she was your ol' lady and insinuated that Sammy was nothing more than a club whore looking to climb a ladder."

"Are you fucking serious?"

"You know I wouldn't lie about that shit, even though I don't trust Melissa as far as I can throw her. I'd bet money Sammy wasn't lying about it, and even more money that she held some shit back."

"Lis really told her she was my ol' lady?" I asked.

"She did, Brother."

"That fucking cunt went too far this time." I tried to sit up a little higher in my bed and immediately regretted that shit as my ribs screamed at me.

"Let me help," Grease offered and moved to the other side of the bed. "If we do this slowly, you should..." His thought cut off as he pushed a button on the side of the rail and the head of my bed raised up higher. It hurt like a motherfucker when my body moved with it, but not as bad as when I tried to do it myself. "That good?" He asked.

I nodded and then turned to Baffle again. "Did you set Sammy straight about that shit?"

"She didn't give me a chance to do that, man."

"You let her go without explaining?" I was fucking pissed. I knew there was no way I could get out of the fucking hospital bed and go after her because my ass couldn't stay awake long enough to get to wherever she had gone.

"You can explain later, when you get out of here. She needed to get out back to her life, Bigfoot. Not to mention, the poor girl hasn't had a shower or clean clothes in days."

"Why didn't any of you take care of her and bring her something?"

"We've had a lot going on, and I honestly didn't think she'd hang in here as long as she did." Baffle dragged a hand down his face and it only then occurred to me how haggard my friend looked. "I know you want her back here, but she needs a little space. She has a lot to process about what went down, and it wasn't happening here while she waited to see if you'd pull through."

"What's that mean?"

"She might not be banged up on the outside like you, but not only did she see you get thrown from your Harley, she also killed a man to keep you alive. That was her first kill. It's going to fuck with her, whether she knows it yet or not."

"Fuck. I didn't even fucking ask if she was okay." I shook

that thought off. "I don't really remember everything that happened that night."

"Understandable," Knuckles interjected. "According to your girl, you were in and out of it when everything went down."

"Sammy," I said and then turned from Knuckles to Baffle, and then across the room to seek out Glitch. "Sammy what? Do we know?"

"Samantha Morton," Knuckles informed me, but the fucker laughed when he said it.

"What's so fuckin' funny?"

"She's been right under our noses for a long time," he answered cryptically. I turned to Baffle for an explanation, but he shrugged.

It was Glitch who finally filled me in. "You know Brady Morton?"

"Went to school with him. He owns the garage we use for the bikes," I stated.

Glitch nodded and waited for me to catch up. Obviously, I was supposed to put something together there. Brady was too young to be Sammy's dad. "She's not married to him," I growled as if saying it would make it not true. My brain felt like mush as I tried to piece everything together. She had been on a date. She wasn't married.

"She's Brady's niece. Lives on the family land and handles their campground and store, plus she works on the RVs when they have issues," Glitch informed me.

"No shit?" I asked as another round of pain meds was dispersed through my I.V. I grinned as the warmth hit my veins and a plan formed in my muddled mind.

"Why is my dad so happy?" My little man asked from the doorway where he stood with Dime.

"Your dad is going to get himself a girlfriend," Knuckles answered with a little chuckle tacked on the end.

"Ew! Girls are gross!"

"You won't think that in a few years, kid," Grease informed my boy, and then my eyes drooped closed.

8. LIGHTS OUT
SAMMY

I drove past the RV and trailer park near the hospital as I headed back to Main Street, and it reminded me of all the duties I'd neglected while I sat in the hospital waiting for a complete stranger to wake up. My family owned a huge chunk of property in Violence, New Mexico. It was not too far across the state line from Arizona, but it felt like a million miles away from where I'd been for the past three days.

Despite knowing that I needed to get back to work, exhaustion beat down on me and I didn't think it was in me to go deal with the campground mess, the camp store, or any repairs that needed to be done to any RVs that were waiting to be serviced. I wasn't sure who my Uncle Brady got to run things in my place. If he was smart, he made my dad and stepmom do something to contribute to the family businesses. My stepmom thought she was above having to work, especially since she had given birth to my baby brother four years ago. My dad had his own business setting up state-of-the-art security for some of the richer landowners and businesses in the state. He often traveled to do so. My stepmother had been a souvenir he brought back from one of those trips.

Since he made really good money with his own business, Dad didn't think he owed any time to what he called the family's "white trash" ventures. He never spoke about us, our family businesses, or land like that before he met Colleen. In fact, if my grandfather was still alive to hear it, he would have made damn sure my dad never saw a penny from the businesses and wouldn't have been allowed to live on the land, either.

My biggest problem with my stepmother was that she kept insisting that she should be the one to move into my grandparent's old house. I've avoided my dad for months because he kept pushing for it to make her happy. They had a perfectly good, three bedroom house for them. It had been just fine for Dad, me, and my mom when she was still alive. It was where I grew up, so I knew it wasn't a hardship for Colleen and her son to live there, especially since she had insisted on completely remodeling it when she moved in with my father. When I first came back from the Army, I no longer recognized it as the house I grew up in.

Then, my grandfather died, and Colleen started her shit about moving into his house because it was bigger. The only problem was that he had left it to me, so that I would have a home to come back to that I could be comfortable with, since Colleen had changed everything about my family's house. The woman had even gone so far as to burn all the pictures left there with my mother in them. I hated her. I tried for my dad's sake when I first came back, but I hated his wife. The only reason I still bothered to force a relationship with any of them was because of my little brother.

It pissed them off that I hadn't moved into the house my grandfather left me and refused to allow them to do so. I wasn't ready to take over my grandparents' house just yet, but that didn't mean I didn't want it. While I worked out what I wanted to do with the house, because it needed some updates, I lived in a cottage near the campground. It made the commute to work a two-minute walk. It also meant that I could take my time, save some money, and really upgrade the house that was meant to be mine without having to live in a perpetual construction zone.

It was almost as though I knew what would be waiting for me when I got home. The way my thoughts drifted to my dad and his new family when I had so many other things to worry about, should have been a sign. When I pulled my car around the dirt road that led up to the campground, I could see Colleen's black Lexus in my driveway. I wanted to laugh because it was coated in a layer of dust again, and I knew that pissed her off. My uncles would not allow for the road into the property or the ones on the property to be paved, as my father's wife continually demanded. They all agreed the upkeep would be too costly and that it wasn't worth it, since the paved portion of the road would be full of dust and dirt after the next windstorm anyway.

I groaned when I realized that the bitch had been lying in wait for me, but I was also in no mood to put up with her shit. I dialed my uncle's phone.

"Brady Morton," he answered. I rolled my eyes, because he was probably too caught up in whatever he was working on to look at his phone before he answered.

"Hey, I need someone at my cabin ASAP."

"Why?"

"The step monster is there waiting for me, and I'm too damn tired to deal with her on my own. Either come be my witness or bring a shovel and be prepared to dig a deep hole."

"Shit. Be right there, kiddo. Take your time. I'll cut across on the side-by-side and meet you there."

"Will do." I hung up and slowed from the seven miles per hour I was doing down to a crawl that didn't even register on my speedometer. I waited until I saw the dust trail Uncle Brady kicked up as he crossed the open expanse of land between the garage where he worked on motorcycles and older cars to the cabin I lived in. Once I knew he would arrive before I did, I picked up my speed.

When I managed to get my truck parked, I could already hear my uncle going off on my stepmother.

"What in the hell are you doing here?"

I got out of my truck and circled around the back where they stood in the drive closest to the cabin I'd been living in. My stepmother was dressed in what amounted to a power suit you might see an executive-level woman in the big city wearing, which was insane because we were in the middle of nowhere, and she was not employed.

"I was waiting for that brat to get home."

"Why? I don't have anything to say to you," I called out to her as I moved closer.

"I had to step in and do your job for you while you were out partying for days on end!" The bitch screeched at me.

"I wasn't out partying. I was at the hospital with a friend."

Brady did a doubletake in my direction at my admission but turned back to Colleen and shook his head. "Sammy hasn't taken a single day off since she came home from the Army. Even if she was out partying, which is none of your fucking business, she has more than earned her time off. I can't say the same for you, though."

"I don't have to work," Colleen retorted with that smug look on her face that always made me wish I could punch her without consequences.

"If you want to continue to live on family land, you do. We let Brian get away with not contributing for too long. There is a stipulation that we each have to work for the family business three days a week minimum as long as we live here, unless there is a medical reason why we can't."

Colleen laughed. "I know for a fact that Brian owns our house outright."

"He might own the house, but he doesn't own the land it sits on. That is part of our family trust that has legal stipulations attached to it. When Joy was alive, she did the work so Brian could focus on his security business. You are supposed to work three days a week in his place as your land rental."

I almost laughed as Colleen sputtered and fumed. "Bullshit!" When she finally yelled, her whole face turned a bright red, nearly purple color.

"Tell your wife the truth," Uncle Brady demanded. We all looked around for my dad. He wasn't there but Brady held his phone up.

I could hear him huff down the line and felt his frustration in that sound. "He's not wrong, Colleen. We are supposed to contribute and I haven't done so for the five years we've been together."

"I don't understand," she mumbled.

"I'll explain it later. Sam?" he called out and I moved so that he could see me on his end of the video call.

"Yes?"

"Who were you at the hospital with?"

"That's really not your business," I shot back. My dad barely had anything to do with me since he hooked up with Colleen. He allowed her to influence him into distancing himself from me, and it wasn't something I was willing to forgive. I had already lost my mom. Because of Colleen's demands and my father bowing to her wishes, it felt like I'd lost my dad, as well. He was nothing more than a stranger to me.

"I knew she was lying!" Colleen shouted triumphantly. Her "gotcha" moment was shot all to shit in the next couple minutes, though.

"Sammy, I heard some things, baby girl. Need to know if they're true. Who were you with?"

"I helped a man who was in an accident and stayed at the hospital in Springerville with him until he woke up," I admitted.

"Bigfoot?" Uncle Brady asked. I nodded, shocked that he knew the man had been hospitalized, not that he knew him. They were around the same age. "Shit," my uncle groaned. Dad remained quiet.

"Do you know what you're doing getting mixed up with the Kings of Anarchy?" my dad asked.

"Getting mixed up with them?" I questioned. "I saved the guy's life and made sure he was going to pull through. I wouldn't exactly call that 'getting mixed up'." I shot back at him. "And even if I was, again, I don't know what business it is of yours."

"I'm your father," he insisted.

"Funny, Brian, but the only man who has behaved like a father to me in the past five years is your little brother. You stopped loving me as your daughter and giving a shit the minute your little fling got knocked up and told you to."

"Sammy, that's about enough."

"You're right, it is. Tell your wife to get the hell off my part of the property because I don't want her here."

"You have to go to work, you ungrateful little bitch!" Colleen snapped at me.

"Ungrateful? Who the hell am I ungrateful to? You haven't done a damn thing for me to be grateful for."

"I worked your damn job the past two days."

"Boo-fucking-hoo, Colleen. You're supposed to put in your share. I've been working seven days a week for the past two years because you wouldn't pull your weight around here. You can fuck all the way off!" I turned back to the phone and glared down at it because I wanted my dad to feel the weight of my words. "Get your wife off my property, and so help me God, if she gets in my business again, comes near any of my property, or so much as whispers in my direction, I will not be held responsible for how I respond to that threat! She has five minutes and I already started the timer."

I turned my back and walked toward the cabin that I'd called my home for the past couple years. I didn't bother to look back, to tune in and listen to what Brady or my dad had to say. I didn't care what Colleen had to say, either. I opened my cabin up, stepped inside, and then shut and locked the door behind me. My family was complicated, my feelings toward them more so. I loved my dad - the man who was there for me while I was growing up, anyway. The man who he became after my mom died and he married Colleen was a different story.

I quietly moved through my cabin, grabbed a protein bar on my way through the kitchen, choked it down, snagged some fresh clothes out of my closet, and then went to take the mother of all showers. Once I was cleaned, I crashed on my bed and was out like a light before my head even hit the pillow.

9. FIND HER
BIGFOOT

"Am I in danger of dying?"

"Well, no, but we don't want you to impede your recovery by leaving too early. You might not realize it, but you've been on some pretty heavy duty pain killers, and they can make you feel like you're a lot better off than you really are."

"I'm not staying in this hospital another fucking day. An hour is too long."

"We know where she is," Baffle said to me as the doctor all but ran out of the room to get my paperwork started.

"I know you do, but she doesn't know that I'm coming for her. Melissa made her think that I have a woman."

"What are you afraid of, man? Think she's going to run off and marry the first man she sees in an attempt to get over you?"

"I'll fucking kill him. She's mine. You know how it is for the men in my family. She's the one."

"Then we'll make sure you get to her as soon as humanly

possible. Sit back and relax until the doctor comes back with your papers. It will give me time to get a cage here to pick you up."

"Fucking hell. How is my baby?"

"I'm sorry to say that your baby is down for the count, but she might have some parts that are salvageable if you want to do a custom build with her."

I shook my head. "Just scrap her. Putting any piece of my wrecked bike on a new one feels like bad luck."

"Maybe it would be good luck. That wreck brought Sammy into your life."

I stopped to think about it for a few minutes and then shook my head again. "Nope. The bike can go. I'll get a new one as soon as my arm heals. Sammy can be my good luck. Gonna put her on the back of my bike as soon as I'm able to ride again." I struggled to get my boots on my feet but refused to ask Baffle for help. As I did, I felt the energy drain right out of me. Fuck, getting boots on my feet shouldn't completely drain me.

"Maybe you should listen to the doctor and stick it out another day, just to be..."

"If you say 'just to be safe' I'm gonna knock your teeth down your damn throat. Since when do any of us play it safe?"

"Just a suggestion considering all the color drained from your face when you bent over to try to get your fucking boot on, you idiot." Baffle leaned down and tugged my boot over my foot and then laced it up. "These fuckers saved your toes, but they look like the road ate the shit out of them."

"I'd say I don't know how I made it out without more

damage, but swear to fuck, Baf, it was because my guardian angel was there that night."

My asshole friend laughed at me. "You know she didn't do anything to help you out, right?"

"She shot a man before he could kill me," I reminded him.

"Yeah," He waved that off. "I meant, she didn't really give you any first aid or whatever. She checked to make sure you were breathing and told me what she thought might be wrong with you, so I could pass it on to Doc."

"She was there. I kept fighting to come back to her voice over and over again when I would slip."

"Yeah, okay, I guess that's something."

"It's everything. You might not understand now, but one day you're going to meet a woman who is going to click for you, and you'll see what I'm talking about."

We sat quietly after that and waited for the doctor to bring back my discharge papers. The coward never showed. He sent the nurse instead.

I was back at the clubhouse less than five minutes before Glitch came to find me in the office. "I knew you wouldn't want to wait on this," he suggested as he flicked a folder on my desk. I got ready to open the file he had gathered about Sammy when a prospect called out a warning.

"Incoming: Melissa and Hawk!"

I slid the file into the top drawer of my desk and looked up just as the door flew open. Melissa stood there looking smug as my boy ran to me. Baffle caught him before he could leap into my lap. "Whoa there, little man. Your dad might be out of the hospital, but he's still hurt right now. You can't jump on him. He might break." I didn't miss the pissy look he threw to my boy's mom. She should have talked to him about that shit before they even walked through the door.

"Shit! Sorry, Dad."

"Language!" Melissa chastised. I pretended not to see my son roll his eyes at his mother because I didn't have the energy to deal with it.

Baffle might have been right about staying in the hospital another night. They had better pain meds there than I did here. What they sent me home with wouldn't touch the pain that had already started to make me nauseous. It didn't matter. There was shit to handle, my kid to see, and my woman to hunt down. The loyalty she showed to me, when I was owed none, was the biggest reason I knew she was it for me. The fact that she worked with my brothers to get me care instead of going against their orders was another. There was also the fact that she was beautiful and had a sassy little attitude that made my dick painfully hard.

I needed to get to Sammy, but I had to reassure my son first and deal with his mom's bullshit, since she was at the clubhouse.

"You know, I had things to do today," Melissa spit out. Every head in the office spun in her direction, including my son's.

"Glitch, take Hawk to get some snacks. I'm sure he's hungry. Kid has a bottomless pit for a stomach."

"Sure thing."

"But I want to see you!" My son whined.

"G-maw Tilly made her special brownies," I told him. "They're in the kitchen."

"Let's go, Glitch!" my kid cried out as he grabbed my brother's hand and attempted to haul him out of my office. Glitch chuckled as he followed behind my son. Melissa stomped her fucking foot.

"I didn't bring him all the way over here just to go eat brownies with one of your club brothers. I brought him to visit you."

"And we're gonna have a little chat that my son shouldn't hear. Sit the fuck down, Melissa."

When she looked as though she might refuse, Baffle stepped closer to her. Melissa finally took me seriously and flung herself into a chair in front of my desk. "What the hell do you want?"

"I want to know why the fuck you thought it was okay to tell Sammy that you're my ol' lady."

"Are you serious right now?" Melissa stood up and dropped her hands to her hips before she thought better of it and flailed them about as she spoke. "This is what you're trying to hold me hostage in your office for?"

"No one is holding you hostage," I growled.

"Oh good, then I'll go grab my boy and leave."

"Sit the fuck down!" I yelled as I came to my feet and stabbed a finger from my good hand down toward the chair. "You're going to answer my fucking question, Lis, and you better make it the fucking truth!"

"I didn't mean anything by it. She's a stranger, a nobody. It looked like she was hanging around to take advantage of you, and then I brought our son there. What if she hurt him or said something to upset him? Hawk was already suspicious of her when we got to your room. I didn't want her to say something that confused him. I didn't want you to wake up and maybe not have memories and have her take advantage of you."

"Do you think Baffle would have left her alone with me if there was any fear of her being a threat?"

Melissa's color-contact enhanced blue eyes shifted toward my VP and back to me. "I didn't know what all he had going on. Sometimes things slip through the cracks when you guys are all up in your club business."

"You saying I can't take care of my club and my prez?" Baffle asked.

"No, it's just..." Melissa stood again. "Look, I did it to protect you and our son. I'm sorry, okay? There were better ways to handle the situation, and I didn't do that because telling her that I was your ol' lady seemed like the easiest option to get rid of her while I had Hawk there to visit you."

A knock sounded on the door before I could put Lis in her place. "What?" I called out. The door opened and our youngest prospect, Reece, stepped inside.

"Sorry, Prez. There's an important call on the clubhouse line, and I think you should take it personally."

"What the fuck now?" I asked as I reached over and picked up the phone. Glitch thought it would be funny to put in a landline, but not only that, he put in an old-school business landline that had several lines that could be transferred to different parts of the clubhouse. No one said anything as I answered, "Bigfoot."

Baffle laughed at me as I glanced up at the prospect who

leaned over my desk and clicked the button for line two. "The one that's lit up, Prez."

"Fuck's sake," I grumbled.

"Hello?" A man's voice called down the line.

"This is Bigfoot," I told him.

"This is Brady Morton. Pretty sure you know who the fuck I am, so I'm going to get right to the point. We have a problem out here at Morton Motors Campground. Sammy just took a guy out."

"On a fucking date?" I asked before he could finish.

"No asshole. She took him out in a permanent kind of way we shouldn't discuss on the phone. No doubt that this is linked back to your club, considering he's wearing a cut of his own."

"Which MC?"

"Mojave Devils."

"Son of a..." I slammed my fist down on the desk. "We'll be right there. Do not let anyone else near her, Brady. Not a single fucking soul until I get there."

"Yeah, we're going to have a conversation about that shit later. You trying to claim my niece?"

"Like you said, later." I hung up and stood. "Get out. Leave Hawk here with Glitch if you have shit to do. Take him with you if you don't. Tell him I'll see him later."

"What's more important than your son?" Melissa asked in her haughty tone.

"Nothing is more important than him, but seeing as he is alive, well, cared and accounted for, there isn't an issue. Now, be a part of caring for him or get the fuck out. I have club business to handle."

"I'll have Jester bring the van around," Baffle announced.

Fucking hell. I was going to have to show up with my competition in his fucking murder van as he cleaned up after another body Sammy dropped because of her involvement with me.

10. ANOTHER CORPSE
SAMMY

Something jarred me awake.

Truthfully, I wasn't sure how long I'd been knocked out. All the action and then the restless, fitful little bit of sleep I got in that uncomfortable-as-hell chair in the hospital left me completely drained when I got back. Then there was the whole confrontation with my step monster. I truly hated that woman and didn't understand what my father saw in her. She was nothing like my mother.

Another sound caught my attention, and I slowly slid out of the bed as I grabbed the gun I kept in the top drawer of my nightstand. I rolled down to the floor, gun in hand, and listened intently. It was hard to hear other noises over the sound of my own frantic heartbeat, but there it was again. The slightest bump and scrape as the front door to my cabin was forced open. Son of a bitch, someone had broken in. I had to hope that it was just one person, because I wasn't sure I'd make it out alive if several people had been sent to take me out.

I stayed absolutely still as I thought about the past two

days since I'd come home from sitting by Bigfoot's side in the hospital. There hadn't been any sign of another person hanging around the property besides the one Colleen checked in. In fact, there were less people overall at the campground thanks to Colleen's attitude with the campers. I hadn't really checked on the remaining two since I'd been back home. Mostly, it was because I was mourning the loss of all those fantasies I'd had of me and a ruggedly handsome biker-man. The lack of sleep while by his side was the other reason. It was kind of scary how drained I felt.

That was before a boatload of adrenaline hit my system. I pulled my cell phone out of my pajama pants pocket and dialed Uncle Brady.

"Sammy?" he questioned.

"Someone broke into my cabin. No cops. Need backup, though. Maybe." I didn't wait for him to respond because the floor squeaked just outside my bedroom door. I waited, crouched on the far side of my bed, until the door burst open and three quick shots were dropped into my bed where I'd been asleep just moments ago. I popped up and fired two rounds, then dropped back down because I didn't know if there would be another body behind the one I'd just dropped.

What if he's wearing body armor?

It should have sounded far-fetched to even think of that possibility, but then again, it didn't seem plausible that someone would try to assassinate me while I slept either. Unlike my assassin, I didn't have a silencer on my gun, so those shots rang out loud and proud. My ears were ringing a little as I carefully peeked around the end of my bed. The man was down and had already spilled a significant pool of blood on my hardwood floor. That would probably leave a stain.

I heard an engine outside and figured it was my uncle, but I slowly moved out from behind my bed and started toward the body on the floor. There was no need to check on the asshole. He was deader than dead.

"Sammy!" I heard Uncle Brady yell through my front door.

"Wait!" I yelled and then quickly cleared the rest of the cabin before I allowed him to come inside. It didn't take long. The cabin was small, one bedroom, one bathroom, and a living room kitchen combo that totaled less than 600 square feet. Once I was sure there was no one else lying in wait, I went to the door and pulled it open.

"What the hell happened? Are you okay?" My uncle's frantic voice as he pulled me into a tight hug made my heart squeeze. I wasn't sure my own dad would have reacted the same way. I could only imagine annoyed indifference from him.

"I'm okay. The guy who came to kill me in my sleep? Not so much."

Brady set me to the side and marched back to my bedroom. He stopped just short of the body, and I saw when he noticed that my bed had a few new holes in it. "What the fuck? Sammy, he shot you!"

"No, he shot my bed. Luckily, it wasn't breathing before he shot it."

"You could have been in that bed. Why weren't you in it?"

I made my way to Brady and wrapped my arms around him again. "I'm okay. I heard something and hid beside the bed with my gun. As soon as I had a clear shot, I took it." I pointed down to the body that continued to pump blood onto my floor. "Look, he's dead. I'm not. The only worry I have now is how the hell I'm going to clean this up. I've never really put a lot of thought into how to dispose of a body before. I mean, I've had plenty of fantasies of taking Colleen out, but the dream is of ending her, not the cleanup afterward." It was a long-winded ramble that left my uncle looking a little shocked.

"You're not okay." He glanced down at the body and then back up at me. "You said no cops, but sweetheart, we have to call someone."

"The club," I muttered.

"The club?"

I nodded. "Bigfoot, Baffle, Jester..." I thought about that for a minute. "Probably Jester, he has a murder van that will be perfect for this."

"What the fuck?" Brady asked before he took hold of my arms and shook me a little bit. He was gentle about it, but it was still jarring. "A murder van?"

"I doubt it's really a murder van, but he did use it to clean up the last body I dropped."

"The last body... Sammy, what in the hell is going on?"

"Call the Kings of Anarchy and have them send someone. This is no doubt linked to the assassination attempt on their president. Besides, they owe me for saving his bacon last time."

I watched as Brady called the clubhouse number, spoke to someone and then spoke to another person. Once he was done, he hung up and pulled me back into his arms as he walked us over to the couch to take a seat and wait. My phone rang as we both let out a long breath and relaxed back into the couch.

"Sam Morton," I said into my phone.

"Hi, this is Cricket and Bobby from site 4." That's all she said.

"Yes?" I prompted.

"Well, we thought we heard gunshots and got worried. These RV walls are thin and they ain't stopping bullets."

"Nothing to worry about, Cricket. I shot a rattlesnake trying to crawl into my cabin."

"A rattlesnake? I didn't know you had rattlesnakes on the property."

"It's not like we can stop nature from happening."

"No, no. I get that. What kind of rattlesnake?"

"Mojave," I said without thinking.

"I thought they were in Arizona."

"We see them sometimes in New Mexico." That wasn't entirely true, at least not as far north as I was. "We had a regular old Arizona black rattler." Honestly, it was a pretty apt description of the asshole lying dead in my bedroom doorway. He was dressed all in black, which was dumb in a desert, since he wouldn't blend with anything like that.

"Oh, okay. Well, wait, aren't they from Arizona too?"

"You do realize we're less than twenty minutes from Arizona, right?"

"Oh, that makes sense. Sorry to bother you." It sounded like Cricket meant to hang up but missed the button. "Bobby, we need to pack up and get out of here. They have a rattlesnake problem here."

"We're in the freaking desert, Cricket. Of course there's rattlers."

At least Bobby had some common sense.

"We need to leave. I'm not comfortable with rattlers committing home invasions."

I hung up my cell. "Me either, sister."

"What was that about?"

"Campers heard the gun and got worried. I think we'll lose at least one, if not both of our current campers."

"Well, hell, I hate to say this, but it might be for the best if we have a snake problem," He tipped his head toward the body on my floor.

"Yep."

Blue lights flashed outside my cabin and my heart rate kicked back into overdrive. "You've got to be kidding me! Who the fuck called the cops?"

"I don't know but stay calm and remember that you do not have to let them in without a warrant."

"Good to know, since there's a fucking dead man on my floor," I whisper-hissed back to my uncle.

"Use my shot to shit blanket and cover him up or something."

Uncle Brady gave me a look that said if the sheriff saw a bloody blanket on the floor, he would definitely ask questions, but whatever. It made me feel marginally better about shit to not have to look at the asshole assassin.

I moved to my door and quickly took a step outside and closed the door behind me again. "Evening, officer."

"Sheriff," he corrected.

Dick!

"What can I do for you?"

He craned his neck around, as if trying to look to see what I was hiding. "I came by to check in with you about the accident again. It felt like there was something you left out of your statement."

"Nope. What I said is exactly what happened. This is kind of a weird time to be out taking witness statements for a vehicular accident when a statement was already made isn't it?" I questioned.

"I had other things to handle throughout the day. We get to things when we can."

"Uh-huh. Well, I have nothing to add to my statement."

"That may be, but I have questions to ask. Follow up, you see. Why don't we go inside and get comfortable?"

"No."

"What do you mean, 'No'?" I could see by the tension in his shoulders and face that he was about to lose his temper, but that didn't stop me from getting downright sarcastic and rude with him.

"Well, 'no' is a two-letter word consisting of the letters 'N' and 'O'. It signifies the lack of consent to do a thing that is asked of a person. Since I already gave my statement, I have nothing else to add and I certainly am not inviting you into my home."

"And why is that?"

"Because I don't like you and I don't have to," I told him.

"Now, you listen here..."

I shook my head. "No, you listen, Sheriff Estes. You're on my land, demanding entry to my house, and I am relatively certain you do not have a warrant to be in either place. You could have called and told me to come on down to the station and give a better statement, during normal hours, but you didn't. You came here at dusk," I pointed down to my pajamas, "when I was about to go to sleep because I'm exhausted from studying for upcoming exams, and you want to question me about something I have nothing more to add to. Did you catch the trucker who almost killed that man?"

"No, we're still unsure who the trucker was."

"Right. So, you haven't even done your job that well, and you want to come here and see if I can do it for you?"

We both turned as the sound of motorcycles and other vehicles echoed up from the road that wrapped around my family's property and would eventually bring them to my cabin. A smug smile bloomed on Sheriff Estes' face. He would have been a handsome man with golden-brown skin, dark hair, and eyes that were a golden brown to match. His personality being that of a dipshit frat-bro on a power trip ruined the appeal, though.

"Thought you weren't affiliated with bikers?"

"I'm not," I offered with a quick shrug of my shoulders. "Maybe they're stopping by to thank me for taking care of their president when he got into an accident. I don't know. I'm not a damn mind reader." I pointed to my pajamas again. "And like I said, I was getting ready for bed when your blue lights disturbed me."

11. WORLD OF HURT
BIGFOOT

As soon as we pulled up outside the tiny cabin Sammy called home, I turned a sharp glare on Sheriff Estes. We all knew that fucker was corrupt as they come, and I didn't like the fact that he was at Sammy's place, especially since her uncle called us for help.

"Is there a problem here?" I asked as Jester got out of the van and Baffle, Grease, and Dime all got off their motorcycles. They came with me to help Sammy, but also as backup in case anyone else was lurking around. Not only did we need a show of force, for Sammy's sake, but we needed to be cautious about moving around without backup too, considering what happened to me.

"Could ask you the same," Estes drawled slowly. "Thought she wasn't affiliated with your gang?" It was a question, not a statement and one that was liable to land the asshole in the dirt.

"Just got released from the hospital earlier today. Saw my kid, now I came to make sure I properly thanked the woman who saved my damn life."

"And you had to bring all of them with you?"

"Safety in numbers," I explained while I wore what I knew to a be an evil fucking grin. "Never know when an eighteen-wheeler might throw a tire up and take a person out." I stared Estes down hard and dared him to say a word.

"Well, be that as it may, you'll have to pay your respects another day. I was just about to re-interview Samantha about your accident."

"No, you weren't." Sammy told him as she crossed her arms over her chest in defiance. Fuck, I needed to get her riled up more often and in private. The way her arms were positioned worked to push her tits up and out further. A smack to the back of my head let me know I'd been caught drooling over her rack. Truthfully, I don't think anyone could blame me, though. She was wearing a tight little ribbed tank and her nipples begged for attention.

"Sammy, you might want to go grab a sweater," I told her as it became obvious that Sheriff Estes also noticed what I'd been looking at. His eyeballs were glued to her tits the same way mine had been before Baffle smacked some sense into me.

"I'm not cold, I'm pissed."

I didn't get to argue with her as Brady Morton walked out of her cabin like he didn't have a care in the world and handed her a sweatshirt. Just my fuckin' luck it was the one Jester put on her at the hospital. The fucker chuckled under his breath, and I turned my glare on him.

"You can't do a damn thing about it in your condition," he taunted under his breath.

"What are you doing here?" Estes asked Brady.

"On my property?" Brady asked and threw his arms

across his chest in much the same way his niece had, only no one stared at his tits.

"You know damn well what I mean. This is Ms. Morton's residence. What are you doing here, if she was supposedly just about to go to sleep."

"Came by to fix her water heater." Brady tipped his head toward Sammy. "She was going to take a shower before bed but couldn't get the damn thing to heat up." He shrugged. "Now, I'm wondering why the fuck you're here." His question was pointed at the sheriff, but then he turned in my direction. "That goes for you guys, too."

"Just here to say our thanks to your niece for doing a stranger a kindness that probably saved my life."

"You're welcome to come in for a few minutes, but my niece has had a tough couple of days studying after taking time off, so you need to make this visit short."

I nodded my agreement as the men started to shuffle into the cabin. Estes tried to go in and I put a hand on his shoulder to hold him back. "Don't think that invite extended to you."

"Get your fucking hand off me!" he spat then turned on Sammy. "We will get another statement from you," he told her.

"No need. My statement hasn't changed. If you feel the need to press the issue further, I will involve my lawyer."

I heard him hiss, "Fuck," under his breath before turned and walked back to his car. The boys made sure not to block the fucker in. I stood and watched as he left and continued to watch as he tried to idle just around the bend. I stood and pointedly stared at the man until he finally got the hint and took off. We watched him go all the way to the end of the private road owned by the Morton family. I stuck my head in the front door. "Prospect, get out here and keep a lookout. Make sure the sheriff doesn't double back around and keep an eye out for anyone else who might be lurking around."

"Yes, Prez."

The little shit was only 18, but he'd do his job because he wanted to impress his dad who was one of the old-timers with the club. The kid was the result of Mickey fucking around on his ol' lady one too many times and a club whore who was determined to earn a patch from a brother. It did not go the way she wanted. Mickey's ol' lady tried to kill him when she found out he had a kid with a club whore. She ended up in prison and Mickey threatened to put the whore in the grave if she came around him. It was only recently that Mickey started to have anything to do with the son who was in the middle of all the chaos, and the minute he showed interest, the kid latched on to the club like we were the glue that would hold his pieces together. It was yet to be seen if he'd make it as a brother or if his desperate need to be accepted would make it impossible to bring him on as a member.

After he was in a spot where he could see the road from both sides, I made my way into the cabin and locked the door behind me. Sammy stood there in front of the body with her head cocked to the side and then heaved out a giant sigh. "He completely ruined this floor."

That was not what I expected. I wasn't alone in that assessment. Jester groaned and then turned toward me. "Please, tell me you changed your mind." I shook my head immediately.

"Not on your life, fucker."

Sammy turned and smiled at the dead man who used to be my friend. Not the corpse, the other soon-to-be dead man, Jester. "I hope you brought the murder van!" I laughed because her voice had a cheery quality to it that should have seemed out of place, all things considered. Apparently, death and murder didn't affect my woman the way it did most people.

"You're not all there, are you?" Baffle asked her.

She pointed down at the guy she had shot. "Do you want me to feel bad for him? That asshole put three bullets into the bed I'd been in a few seconds before. If I hadn't heard him breaking in the front door, I would be the corpse getting cleaned up. Fuck that. In a game of him or me... I chose me, and it makes me happy that it worked out the way I wanted it to."

I glanced from Sammy to her uncle who stared at his niece like he wasn't sure they had ever met before. "I'm beginning to wonder if you lied about what you did in the Army."

She cocked her head to the side and rolled her eyes at him, as if he was nothing more than a nuisance. "Really?" She turned to me then. "Sorry about the mess. I'd have taken care of it myself, but honestly, I have no clue what to do with a dead body. Besides," She pointed down to his cut. "I think that piece of leather means him being here was tied to you somehow."

"Maybe, but my guess is they got your name off the accident report and figured since I was incapacitated, it had to be you who offed their Road Captain."

"Did they find his body?" She asked.

"Hell no. There's nothing to find. It just makes sense if he never came back that it was because someone took him out first."

"Now there's a second man who will be missed, and he was associated with my niece," Brady said. Then he shook off whatever thought he must have had and looked me in the eye. "There's more to this, Trav."

"You two know each other?" Sammy asked.

"Went to school together," her uncle explained as I watched to see if it bothered her that I was the same age as one of her uncles. He was the youngest of the three Morton boys, but still there was at least a decade between Sammy and me, maybe more. I wasn't sure how old Sammy was because it really didn't matter to me. I knew she was an Army vet, so she had to be over the age of eighteen, and the way she carried herself told me she was probably closer to mid-twenties. Then again, there was the comment about her studying for an exam earlier. Fuck, I didn't know shit. It made me angry with Melissa all over again for interrupting shit when I had a file on Sammy in my hands earlier that would have answered all my fucking questions.

"What did you mean when you said there's more to this?" I finally asked.

"I checked the security cameras while Sammy was talking to Sheriff Estes. We have them up near both garages, the campground, and inside and outside the camp store."

"Was there someone else here?"

Brady shook his head, not this time. "The Sheriff showed up at a rather convenient time, considering how quickly that happened after the attempt on Sammy's life. While shady as fuck, that wasn't what bothered me the most."

"What did?" Baffle asked him.

"Patrick," Brady acknowledged my VP by his government name. "My sister-in-law had to take over at the camp store while Sammy was gone. I also had her stay on in the days since Sammy returned, because I gave my niece a couple of extra days off to get herself straight and get some studying in. Colleen was reluctant to do the job, and that's putting shit mildly."

"You think she pulled some shit out of resentment?"

Brady shook his head, and the grave look he lobbed on his niece made the hairs on the back of my neck stand on end. "What the fuck did she do?"

Instead of telling us about it, Brady pulled out his phone and queued up video footage from earlier in the day. It was the same man who was dead on the floor. The way he spoke with Colleen, and she with him, seemed very familiar. As in, they had not just met. That point was proven further when she told him exactly where to find Sammy and that they might need to move up their timetable if he offs the girl.

My phone buzzed as we watched Colleen flirt and drive a proverbial bus over her own stepdaughter. She pointed to the cabin where Sammy lived as I picked up my phone.

"Bigfoot." Everyone turned to me and Brady paused the video.

"Hey Prez, I had some news that couldn't wait. Ran a deeper dive on Colleen. Seems she might have an uncle in the Mojave Devils. There's a discrepancy with their names that threw me off a bit, and I'm looking into that, but she has him listed as her next of kin at a hospital in Arizona."

"How in the hell did you get that information?" I asked.

"It's better if you don't ask. If the body your girl dropped happens to be another Devil, I wanted you to know sooner rather than later that there might be a fox in the henhouse over there."

I ignored Glitch's need to make everything about predator-prey animal relations, thanked him, and hung up. "Looks like Glitch just figured out why stepmom was so fucking comfortable with a Mojave Devil."

"What's going on?" Sammy asked.

"She has an uncle in their MC. Glitch said something about her name being different and it threw him. He's checking into everything, but her next of kin contact is a member of the fucking MDMC."

Baffle was far too quiet about everything as he stood there staring at his own phone. Eventually, he glanced up at us, and I knew the minute our eyes connected that the shit we stumbled into with the Mojave Devils was about to get deeper.

"Fucking Devils hit our West Texas Chapter."

"Who?" I barked the one-word question.

"Rio's girl."

"Didn't know Rio had a girl," Jester said.

"His friend, Issy was taken."

"What more do we know?" I asked Baffle.

He shook his head. "Not much. Promised to get Glitch on it ASAP. Need to get Dime back to the clubhouse with me."

"Go! I'm staying until the mess is cleaned up here."

"I'm staying to help Jester. This is going to take more than one person," Grease inclined his head down to the dead body that still littered the floor.

"I can help with the cleanup," Sammy offered. "It's my mess anyway."

Jester moved closer to my girl and patted her shoulder. "No, we don't want you getting too close to him. If, on the off chance, his body is discovered before we can work our magic on it, we don't want any more evidence transferring to it that will point someone in your direction. Have a good feeling the sheriff was here earlier because he knew what was going down tonight. He wanted verification that either you were dead or the reason why you weren't. They'll be looking for him."

"I agree with Jester. We need to keep you as far from the body as possible."

"He's in my house. I think being concerned about trace evidence leading him back to me is a moot point." Sammy rolled her eyes, but I reached over and pulled her back into my arms and held her there. To my surprise, she didn't try to pull away.

"Be a good girl and stay back while my men clean this shit stain off your floor, yeah?"

Sammy shivered in my arms but gave a quick nod and turned her head to the left so she could see me.

"Be a good boy and help them then, so they can get out of here quicker." I grinned down at her and leaned in like I might kiss her, but the minute I saw panic flare in her eyes, I reached up and bopped her nose with my finger instead.

"Park your ass out of the way." I glanced up at Brady then. "You too, Uncle Brady."

"Don't fucking call me that, asshole."

I laughed and moved to help my men get the mess cleaned up. Sammy was right about the floor. There was no helping it. "Gonna need a rug or something to cover this up for now."

BY THE TIME everything was cleaned up, Brady decided to go with Jester and Grease to dispose of the body. It wasn't something we'd normally allow. Seeing as how it was his niece's kill, he wanted to be damn sure that it was done properly, and I couldn't see keeping that shit from him. He had enough skin in the game we didn't have to worry about him possibly giving us up.

"How are you going to get back?" Sammy asked me when the van took off without me.

"I'll call for another ride if I need one. Right now, I don't think you should be left alone, especially not while you're sleeping."

"I heard the last guy."

"You did, but you weren't coming down off an adrenaline high then. It changes things. You crash out harder and pick up on less external shit while your body dives into recovery mode." I took hold of Sammy's hand and pulled her toward the bedroom. When we got to where the body had been, I bent down and braced my good arm under her ass and hauled her over the stain on the floor.

"No! Stop. You can't." I groaned as she slipped out of my hold and took a step back.

"Fuck, I shouldn't have done that."

"No shit! Did your parents drop you on your damn head as a kid?"

"It's possible," I admitted sheepishly as I tried to remember how to breathe with my ribs screaming at me.

"Maybe I should talk to your mom about how much damage she did. I hope she feels bad that her son is an idiot now. Did you pop a stitch or a bone or maybe a lung?"

I started to laugh until that shit hurt, too. "No laughing," I wheezed.

"Sorry, do I need to call someone? Your doctor, the club doc guy, or maybe your mom?" she asked sincerely, then she chuckled. "Maybe not your mom since she probably caused this with all the traumatic brain injuries from your childhood."

"Stop!" I choked out as I held tight to my ribs. Fuck, this woman could make me laugh with my whole chest as the damn thing rattled apart.

"Let me see," Sammy insisted as she kneeled in front of me and tugged my cut open and shirt up. After a minute of just staring at my chest, she glanced up at me from a position that made my cock weep. "I don't know why I did this because I have no clue what I'm looking at." She slowly rose in front of me and my hands immediately wrapped around both sides of her face as I pulled her toward me for a kiss.

At the last second, just as our breaths danced together and lips were about to touch, she yanked back from my hold. "No! You have an ol' lady at home waiting for you and a kid with her. I might be a killer, but I'm not a cheater."

"You're neither. Both those kills were self-defense." Sam stood there staring at me like I'd lost my mind. "You're not a killer just because you protected yourself. That makes you a survivor. Period." She turned her back to me and walked over to the bed where she started to strip the sheets. "Listen up, Sammy." It was an order, and I didn't care that she continued her task and threw the fucked-up sheets away only to examine the bullet holes in her mattress. "I do not have an ol' lady. I haven't even been with Melissa since she got pregnant with Hawk. She made that shit up. I don't fucking know why. She claims she did it to protect me but trust me when I tell you it has already been made very clear to her that I don't need her form of protection."

Sammy got on her knees again, though not in front of me. She scurried under the bed with her ass in the air for a moment, and I groaned in frustration as that biteable little peach of hers was thrust up. Her little sleep shorts left nothing to the imagination as they pulled tight.

"What the fuck are you doing?" Her ass dropped down as she flattened herself onto her belly and crawled forward under the bed a little further.

"All three bullets are embedded into the floor. Looks like I'll have to replace the whole room, not just the stained section."

"I'll take care of the cost. This shit happened because you stopped to help me. Now, I need to know that you heard me and believed what I just told you."

As Sam shimmied back out from under bed, she turned and looked at me for a solid minute before she nodded her head. "I believe you. She seemed like the type who might pull something like that. Still, you need to get something straight, just because I think you're fuck-hot doesn't mean anything is going to happen between us."

"Why the fuck not?"

"You're Uncle Brady's age, for one. He's ten years older than me."

"That's nothing."

She sighed and then stuck two fingers in the air. "You

have a kid, and I'm pretty sure he's the same age as my little brother."

"You don't like kids?"

"I don't know the first thing to do with kids, except to corrupt the shit out of them and send them home to their parents. I can't do that if I'm the one at home with Daddy."

I groaned again as she called me "Daddy" and I couldn't even articulate if it was because I liked it or thought it was creepy. Considering she was a full-grown adult, I went with liking it. Maybe a little Dom/sub play would work for us.

"I have a lot to think about, and maybe you do, too. How will your son like having another woman around? He didn't seem too impressed with me at the hospital."

"He just didn't know who you were yet."

"Still, I have a lot going on. Adding an aggressive biker man who has a whole club out to murder him - and me - only adds to it. I'm trying to get my MBA, and I work like seven days a week." She plopped down on her butt at the end of her bed. "And I don't even have a bed to sleep in that doesn't have holes in it. Can you just go? I need time to think about my life and where the hell I'm supposed to go from here."

"Sammy, I don't want..."

"Please, not tonight. I just want to be able to fall apart in private. That," She pointed to the blood stain on her floor, "was the second man I killed in a week. He was actually trying to kill me. The other one was after you. I need to just wallow in my hole-riddled bed with some ice cream and hope like hell that tomorrow turns out way better."

"I'm not comfortable leaving you here alone. What if

they send someone else or the sheriff comes back with a trumped-up warrant?"

"I'll handle it. I'm sure Brady is on the lookout and will be all night."

"Fine, but this conversation is only on hold. We will talk about the future, and what it looks like for us together, the next time I see you." I turned to leave and as I walked away from her room, I heard her mumble, "Fuck me, he's hot and bossy, and I kinda like it."

I grinned the whole way out her door. When I got out there, Brady was waiting for me. "Your boys said you might need a ride back to the clubhouse." He dangled a set of keys in front of me. I shook my head.

"Not leaving. She wants space, and I'm giving her that, but I'll be right here all night."

"Not necessary. I'll look out for her."

"She's in this shit because she helped me. It's my responsibility."

"Why the fuck are *you* in this shit?"

"Your guess is as good as mine at this point. Mojave Devils were never even on our radar until they tried to take me out."

"And they targeted another chapter of your club too?"

"That they did. We have men on it. They'll figure out what the fuck is going on, but until we do and shit is safe for her again, she's going to have eyes on her - ones that I trust. Tonight, that means I'm up for guard duty."

Brady kicked back against the side-by-side he offered me to use to get back to the clubhouse. He tossed the keys to me, and stupidly, I reached up to pluck them out of the air. My ribs tugged and burned in my chest again. "Dammit."

"Yeah, that's what I thought. Looks like we're both sitting guard duty." He patted the side of the tricked-out Polaris and grinned at me. "Take a load off for a minute. It has heat. Gonna be a chilly fucking night. Might as well get comfortable while we can. I have a laptop in there with a security feed pulled up."

"Sounds good."

"It would sound even better if you had one of your prospects run out here with a hot fucking pizza and some drinks. I skipped dinner and I'm hungry as fuck."

"I see you haven't changed much since high school."

"You knew I didn't."

I would have shrugged him off, but it hurt too much to move like that. Instead, I turned and told him the same thing I always did when we had the opportunity to talk. "Still have an open invite to join the club."

"Still thinking on it." It was always his go-to answer. I hoped one day he would take me up on the offer.

12. CHANGING SPACES

SAMMY

I GLARED AT THE BULLET HOLES IN MY MATTRESS AS IF THEY WOULD automatically mend themselves because my brain willed it to be so. It didn't happen, and eventually I grabbed my spare blanket out of the closet, curled up on my naked, hole-filled mattress, under my blanket, and fell asleep. Bigfoot was right about one thing, the crash after the adrenaline rush hit me hard as fuck.

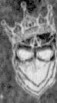

WHEN I WOKE in the morning, I found Bigfoot and my uncle laughing about something as they sat in the Polaris together. It was weird to see them getting along so well until I remembered that they were friends in high school.

"Looks like someone couldn't get a ride home. Don't tell me... Your club brothers don't actually like you."

"Ha, ha." Bigfoot mock laughed at me as my uncle snickered. As if on cue, a van rolled up, and my would-be suitor got out of the Polaris and headed over to his ride. "We're still going to have that talk, Sammy."

"Whatever you say, big guy!"

He grinned up at me and looked like he was about to say something until my uncle butted in. "She's still my niece. Whatever bullshit is about to come out of your mouth can wait until I'm not around."

Bigfoot smirked at me and then hopped in the van. They took off way quicker than I expected. It wasn't until my phone beeped with an incoming message that I realized it bothered me that he left so quickly.

> Bigfoot: Something came up. Have to run to see to some shit at the club. Brady is going to talk to you about something. I want you to agree and call me later when you're free.

I didn't bother to respond to his text and left him on read instead. "What is it that you're supposed to talk to me about?"

"We need to move you into the big house."

"What? Why?"

"Because someone tried to kill you in this one yesterday and we can defend the big house easier. It's at the final stopping point of a dead-end road, we have cameras set up outside that we don't have here, and there's more room in case you need a security detail to stick around with you."

"Absolutely not."

"Sammy, it also has fresh mattresses in three of the bedrooms, and they don't have bullet holes in them."

I huffed in frustration. "Fine, but you know this is going to make the renovations go slower, right?"

"I don't see why it has to. We'll figure out some workarounds and it will be all good."

"Fine, but I'm not taking Nanny and Pop's room. That's just weird. It still smells like someone died in there."

"No, it doesn't. You're just being weird."

"Okay, you sleep in there, then. Let's see how you like it when your parents' ghosts are getting busy in the room while you try to sleep."

"What the fuck is wrong with you? Did you take a bullet to the brain yesterday and forget to tell us?"

I giggled. "Nope, but you clearly didn't understand how weird it would be to sleep in that room until I really made you think about it."

"Yeah, thanks for the glimpse of my parents' afterlife sex life." Brady scratched his head. "Aftersexlife?" He questioned.

"I think you had it right the first time."

"Some days, I really hate that I'm your favorite uncle."

I made a face at him and put my balled up fists up to my eyes in a crybaby motion. Brady flipped me off.

It wasn't until we took the second load of my things over that I noticed something was off. After scanning the living room twice, I finally realized what was missing. "Brady, did you take that grandfather clock out of here?"

"No, why?" He called back from the kitchen.

"It's missing." I turned around just as he barreled into the living room.

"What the fuck?"

"That's not all," I said as I took another slow spin around the room. "The antique pieces have all been replaced."

"Son of a bitch!" Brady seethed the words out as he yanked his phone from his pocket. "That mother fucker is going to bring every fucking piece back here."

"If she didn't sell them already." My heart ached at the loss of all our family heirlooms. It wasn't all of them, but there were a few pieces of furniture that had made the journey from Scotland in the mid-1700s. The Long Case Grandfather Clock had been one of those pieces. "I might just add her to my body count if we can't get that clock back."

"I know." Brady came over and wrapped an arm around my shoulder. He tugged me into his side. "Your dad isn't answering his phone."

"No surprise there. It's like he forgot that we're his family once he married that skank. I wonder what he'll think when he finds out she was okay with pointing a killer in my direction after she flirted with him."

Brady sighed. "Honestly, Sam, I'm not sure we should tell him just yet."

"Why not? He needs to know. If nothing else, he should protect my little brother from that woman. What if she takes him and we never see him again?"

"I have my doubts that your father has a legal leg to stand on there."

My eyes must have widened to twice their normal size. It never occurred to me that my little brother might not be biologically related to me. "That's impossible right? He would have had a DNA test done before he agreed to marry her. I always assumed he would verify that kind of thing. Didn't he?"

Brady shook his head. "I don't think he did. Never saw any proof of it, anyway."

"Well, shit. How long are we supposed to wait?"

Brady pulled me over to the couch that had also been replaced with much cheaper furniture. Once we sat down, he laid it out for me. "I talked to Bigfoot about a lot of things last night and we need to trust that he's working on this. More importantly, he has some pretty tech-savvy members who are digging for all the information they can before we go to your dad."

"What if he's in on it with her."

"Fuck that!" Brady grunted. "No fucking way does my big brother know that his wife tried to kill his daughter. No fucking way. He would never harm you." Brady was frantic as he clutched my shoulders and turned me to face him. "You know your father loves you to the end of this Earth, right?"

My head shook back and forth of its own volition. "I don't know that. Not anymore. He checked out after mom died, and I never really got him back. It's like the part of him who loved me died with her. Maybe I remind him of her too much. Maybe he decided he hated me because I was gone when it happened. I don't know. When I got back from the Army, he already had a new wife and kid."

"I know your dad has been lost for a long time, but I promise that he never stopped loving you, kid."

There was nothing to say to that. My uncle loved his brother. I loved my dad - the one I grew up with anyway. The man he had become since I left for the Army, since my mother died, they were two different people. My faith had been tested and my father found lacking. Case in point - the house we were sitting in. He had been trying to take it from me simply because his wife wanted it and didn't give a damn that it was specifically left to me in my grandfather's will.

Later, as I settled into the bedroom that used to be Uncle Brady's when he was younger, my phone beeped with an incoming text. For a few seconds, I thought maybe it was my dad wondering why I'd moved into the big house. I was only somewhat disappointed to see that it was Bigfoot who texted me. Immediately, I changed his picture from the generic one assigned to new contacts to one of a cartoon Bigfoot.

> Bigfoot: Been thinking about you today.

> Sammy: No need. I haven't even had to use a pea shooter for rattlesnakes today.

> Bigfoot: You're on my mind all the time.

> Sammy: Scandalous, considering you have a whole family.

> Bigfoot: You know that was a bunch of bullshit.

I did know that, but for some reason I liked poking the bear - or maybe I should say, I liked poking the Bigfoot. He seemed to like when I teased him.

Sammy: You'll be happy to hear that I'm all settled in my grandparents' house.

Bigfoot: It's your house.

Sammy: It still doesn't feel like it.

Bigfoot: I want to come keep you company, but I have Hawk with me tonight.

Sammy: He's your priority - as he should be. By the way, you gave him a really cool name.

Bigfoot: How do you know it was me who gave it to him?

Sammy: I've met his mother. She's not that cool.

I laughed as the three little dots that indicated he was typing started and stopped and started and stopped over and over again.

Sammy: Did I throw you for a loop with the truth?

Bigfoot: No, you made me laugh and it hurt like hell. Dropped my damn phone three times.

I giggled at my phone and then sighed because there was no way it was sane to even think about getting involved with the man. I had already killed two people since meeting him and it had only been a week. One very long, very drama-filled week. I felt drained again just thinking about it.

> Sammy: Tired now. Goodnight.

He didn't respond before I flipped my phone over on the bed-side table and closed my eyes. I wasn't sure who was watching out for me, but Uncle Brady had assured me that it was safe for me to go to sleep, and I trusted him, so that's what I did.

13. IT'S NOT STALKING
BIGFOOT

"Headed out?"

Baffle and Knuckles were beside the bar as I made my way by them, headed to the front door. I stopped and turned to see that neither one of them could hold back the smirks. I narrowed my eyes on them. "Why?"

"Just wondering if you're off to see Hawk or setting out on stalker duty." Knuckles couldn't even finish his sentence before he started to laugh.

"You both know why, and it's not stalking!"

"Yeah, but she won't even go out on a date with you. At some point, you might need to throw in the towel on that one."

Baffle knew better. I wasn't throwing in the towel on Sammy. She might not understand just yet, but she would. Eventually. She was being stubborn. That's all there was to it. She still liked to text back and forth with me. We had been dancing around everything for two weeks since it all went down with her second kill. The only times I'd seen her were when I watched over her from the shadows to make sure there wasn't another attempt on her life. It wasn't that I hadn't tried to see my beautiful angel. Sammy just wasn't having it. She didn't feel comfortable dating me when she knew it would pose a problem for the mother of my child and most likely Hawk as well. There was nothing I could say to reassure her and fucking Melissa kept dodging my calls and texts, despite the threats that she better make shit right.

Before I could take off, Dime yelled for me. "What now?" I asked out loud.

"Problem with the garden," he announced. Not everyone that hung around the clubhouse knew about our shroom operation. Most of the time when someone mentioned the garden, everyone assumed we were growing our own weed. We did do that, since we had a legal dispensary. It wasn't attached to the club, we had our legitimate businesses run through shell corporations that appeared to be owned by individuals who couldn't be members of the club. In fact, my mom, Tilly was the one who owned the dispensary. Nadine, Baffle's aunt, officially owned the club's gas station, the V-KOA Fill-Up.

Just as I was about to ask Baffle to take the shroom problem, his phone rang. "Someone just robbed the V-KOA."

"Couldn't have been a local, they all know better."

"Might be related to the MDMC," Baffle suggested.

"Shit. You and Knuckles go handle the V-KOA. Call for Smooth if you need an extra body. I'll handle this shit." I turned and followed Dime to the office where we had a hidden entrance, in addition to the cave system that ran just behind our clubhouse. It ran nearly the length of our property and we long ago closed off any possible points of entry from lands beyond ours, just in case.

"Wait!" I turned to see Knuckles at the door to the office. "What's up?"

"What about Sammy?"

"Fuck," I hissed. "I'll get Kingston on her until I'm done here."

"You sure about that?"

"Why the fuck wouldn't I be?"

"Pretty sure the prospect is closer to her age than you are."

"Fuck off!" I yelled at him as I dialed our youngest prospect. "Need you to follow my girl around today."

"Melissa?"

"Fuck no. That's Hawk's mom, not my girl. Need you to follow Samantha Morton. She lives and works over on the land behind Morton Motors."

"Where we take the bikes to get them serviced?"

"That's it. Sammy works at the campground back there, and she lives at the end of the road that swings around to property."

"Okay, but what do you want me to do?"

"If she leaves the property, follow her. Keep tabs, don't let her know you're there, and for fuck's sake if she spots you, you better tell her you're my prospect before she shoots you."

"Why would she shoot me?"

"She won't so long as you don't get caught tailing her." I chuckled as I heard the kid audibly swallow. "Don't worry kid, just keep her safe and call immediately if you see any bikers not affiliated with our club approach her."

"Okay, Prez. I'm on it."

"Good." I hung up on the kid and followed Dime down into our cavern, shroom grow house.

It didn't take long to see what the emergency was with the mushrooms. There was an entire section of them that had a weird webbing on the caps. "What the hell is this? We have spiders down here?"

"No, I don't know what it is but look over here. It seems like it started here in the back of this section. Not only does it have the webbing but the caps are full of dark spots, and they appear to be dying off."

"Son of a bitch. If this is some kind of disease or virus, we have to worry about the rest of the crop," I said. I turned to look at just how close and closed in the rest of the crops were. "We need someone who knows what the hell they're doing down here and then we need them to train several brothers."

Dime nodded his head as he continued down the row of raised beds. "Losing Twitch fucked us with this stuff."

Twitch had been our mushroom expert. He was the whole reason we added the shroom business to our club. He knew what the fuck he was doing and after two years of careful cultivation on his part, we finally had a crop that net us a huge chunk of profit. We saw our profits soar over the next four years and had huge contracts with sellers across four states. That meant we couldn't afford to lose a single mushroom, never mind the entire section that seemed to be infected. If whatever happened to the section spread to the rest of the mushrooms throughout the cave, we were fucked.

"We need to find someone who can handle this shit."

"Well, it's not like we can take out an ad for a fucking mushroom farmer. That might tip off the fucking cops."

"For now, I want you to get whoever you need to down here to help seal off this section from the rest. Let's hope whatever this is can be contained and that it hasn't already spread down the line too far. Set it up like this section is in a clean room. Plastic walls, whatever the fuck you have to do to minimize the spread. Let's get it done."

"On it," Dime told me as he ran off to the supply room to grab what was needed. Luckily, we kept sheets of clear plastic down here for various reasons. We'd probably have to restock once the barrier walls were put around the infected mushrooms, though.

TWO HOURS LATER, we finally got the plastic wall up, but I wasn't sure if that was enough to keep the other portion of the crop healthy. Something had created the right environment for the section we sealed off to grow fucking webs, or whatever it had done. I worried that it wouldn't be our only loss, despite our efforts. None of us knew enough about the crop to really be effective. If I didn't find someone who knew what they were doing, we would have to drop the mushroom business, and no one wanted that because it was booming. The demand for psychedelics had risen again in the past two years due in part to a fresh study that claimed micro-dosing them could basically cure depression and anxiety or some shit.

I didn't really know the science behind the shit, but when I got ready to look it up online, my phone rang. "Bigfoot," I called down the line even though I knew exactly who it was.

"There's someone following me," Sammy said in a calm tone.

"Who is following you?"

"How the hell should I know? He's young, wearing a leather vest thing like you do, but I can't see the back of it to know who he belongs to."

"What does he look like?" I asked.

"He's tall, maybe a little over six feet. Skinny. Young. He looks like he might still be in high school, if I'm being honest."

"How long has he been tailing you?"

As she answered I shot Kingston a text.

> Bigfoot: Is anyone else tailing my girl, other than you?

> Prospect K: No. She's at the library. Just the librarian, me, and your girl here.

> Bigfoot: Okay, keep it that way, if you can.

"Sammy, where are you?" I asked and she huffed at me.

"Library. I needed to study, and the big house doesn't have internet hooked up right now."

"How the hell do you not have internet? I thought Brady said there were security cameras out there."

"There are security cameras, but they're hardwired into his system somehow. They don't require the internet. You know who does though? Me. I require the internet for research purposes."

"Okay. Stay there, I'm on my way."

"You better hurry before I have to handle your business again."

I chuckled. "Please, don't shoot my prospect."

"Your prospect?" she asked.

"Yes."

"Why is your prospect following me around?"

"He's there to keep you safe because I had something I needed to take care of before I could leave the clubhouse."

"Okay, fine. I guess I'll see you when you get here, then."

"You'll definitely see me, baby. Soon."

I could almost see her roll those beautiful multi-hued eyes at me.

14. PROTECTING MY ASS

SAMMY

My eyes were so tired by the time Bigfoot showed up, I would have agreed to just about anything to get away from the case study I'd been assigned. There was a point where numbers and information started to blend together, and I had reached it about twenty minutes into the supply chain issues that were presented to me. I wanted to get my MBA because I thought it would help me do something more for the family business, especially in the future when it would one day fall on my shoulders to preserve it for future generations.

The more education I got, the less it seemed geared toward my small family business. That most likely my frustration talking, though. Someone cleared their throat and I was startled to see that Bigfoot stood close enough that he could have reached out and touched me before I even knew he was there. I gasped and jumped back a little.

"Now, I know I'm tired," I whispered.

"You were pretty lost in whatever this is that you're doing." He hoisted me up from my chair and wrapped his arms around me and it never occurred to me to fight his hold, even though I still wasn't sure it was the wisest move on my part to get involved with a man whose kid's mother was so close to him that she felt entitled to run other women off. It just didn't seem like a situation I wanted to be involved in, even if part of me did regret that decision.

"This is Kingston," Bigfoot announced. The young guy who had been following me around for a good chunk of the morning stood there with his face tinged slightly pink in embarrassment.

"Don't worry, I'm especially observant, except for when I'm knee deep in a case study."

"Taking my girl for a break, stay here and watch over her stuff. Do not leave unless the building is on fire."

"You got it, Prez," the kid announced. The way he did it made me believe that Bigfoot was not only important to him, but someone the kid respected. The fact that his boss hadn't reamed him out in front of me for failing to go unnoticed in his babysitting duties went a long way to gaining my respect, as well. I had spent a good amount of time wondering what it must be like to run a motorcycle club and what kind of management style a person running one might have.

"Where are we headed?" I finally asked him when we made our way out of the library.

"I thought maybe Jennika's Diner, you know, since we have so many choices here."

I giggled at that because he wasn't wrong. We had two restaurants in our little town, that didn't include the two bars that were owned by the club. One of those restaurants was Smiley's restaurant, which was only open for dinner. Then there was Jennika's Diner, which opened for breakfast and lunch most days and brunch on Sundays. It suited the people of Violence, New Mexico just fine. If we wanted a change of pace, we would drive to a larger town and get our fill of too many bad choices before we headed back to our little space and the just-right options that made us all happy.

It was something I had missed dearly while I was gone in the Army. The other thing that had been missed was the ability to walk from one end of our little town to the other without breaking a sweat. Our climate in Violence was fairly mild year-round and didn't lend itself to the extreme back and forth you got in the desert thanks, in part, to our elevation.

"You do realize that stalking is a crime and we're about to pass the jail, right?" I teased Bigfoot.

"It's not stalking." I could almost hear laughter in his voice as he explained that to me, like it was a familiar conversation. "It's protection."

"Did you rehearse that in the mirror back home?"

Bigfoot swatted my ass. "Quit being a brat." After a minute he shook his head and then chuckled before he put his good arm around my shoulder and pulled me closer to him. "As a matter of fact, I might have had a similar conversation with my VP and Sgt. at Arms earlier."

"Oh! So, I'm not the only person who thinks you're a stalking stalker who stalks me?"

"Okay, brat. You know why I need to keep you safe."

"I know, and while I can joke about it, I appreciate you making sure I don't have to up my body count." His eyes flicked to mine and there was a smolder to them that made me uncomfortable in places I didn't want to mention as we passed Smiley's.

"We're going to up your body count, Sammy. Not the one you were referencing, but I promise you any others before me won't even compare."

"Well, someone's full of themselves." Suddenly, the temperature outside didn't seem mild at all. I might have had my reservations about dating the local MC's president, but that didn't mean I was immune to how he affected me.

As we walked into Jennika's Diner, I decided to deflect back to the original topic of conversation. "I'm not saying I don't appreciate a person looking out for me, but you have to admit it's a little pervy of you to always be lurking outside my bedroom window at night. You might as well be wearing a trench coat with your hands stuffed in the pockets ready to flash me all the goods the minute I look outside."

I hadn't realized that the hostess-slash-waitress had been standing close enough to overhear me until she burst out laughing. "Oh my God! I am so going to tell Lis about that!" She was nearly doubled over from laughing so hard, so I grabbed us a couple menus. "Sorry," the woman managed to get out. "I don't think I'll ever get that flasher image out of my head now." She made sure her attention was on me before she added, "Good luck with this one, especially if he's so fascinated that he's stalking you. You'll never get clear of him now, even if that's what you really wanted."

"Great," Bigfoot grumbled as the woman showed us to our table. "Bring us a couple waters, would ya?" His question was obviously meant to dismiss the woman who was laughing at him, but I had to admire the fact that he did it respectfully. The minute she walked away, I moved to sit down on the side of the table that put my back to the wall and the door in my line of sight.

"Sweetheart, I'm going to need you to trade me places," Bigfoot stated evenly as he stared down at me with a puzzled look on his face.

"Why?"

"It's my job to keep you safe. Part of doing that requires me to be able to see all the entrances, exits, and everyone in the room."

I shook my head as my eyes tracked each window, door, and the people at each table. There was a hallway that led back to another dining area where there were more doors. It was something I would have to keep my eye on.

"I need you to trust me with your safety, Sam."

I turned my gaze up to his. "In order to earn that trust, you need to know what will make me feel comfortable in certain situations. Then, you'll do your best to see that I am afforded that comfort because it is what I need to feel safe. The fact is that I don't trust you yet because you haven't earned it. Forcing me to put my back to the crowd and the doors will keep me on edge the whole time we're here. I won't trust that you have my best interest at heart, and you will not see my best side because I will be too concerned with who might approach on my six."

Bigfoot blew out a breath and then gave one quick nod of his head. Then, he took a seat on the chair beside mine and shimmied the table around just enough that we sat catty-corner facing out toward the rest of the room together. We were both able to see the entire restaurant and have our backs to the wall. "Better?"

I grinned at him. "You earned points for the compromise."

"Never had a woman who didn't want to turn over the burden of her security to me."

"Those women are lucky that they've never had their security shattered so badly that they have to fear doing that." My words came out slightly mumbled, because it hurt to admit that I was flawed in that way.

Bigfoot's hand came down on top of mine, and I jumped slightly at the touch. "Sorry," He hurried to apologize. "I want you to enjoy a meal with me, and it fucking kills me that part of your jumpiness is due in part to my own shit. Never wanted to add to your burden, sweetheart."

"You didn't." He gave me a look that said he knew better. "Obviously what happened with you that night had an impact but so has my other unwanted visitor and the person who sent him to my place."

"I'm fuckin' thankful that you made it through both of those situations. It's also why I'm so fucking protective of you. All of this shit started with me. I don't want you to feel unsafe wherever you go simply because you stopped to help me on the side of the road. It's not even just me feeling responsible for your safety after putting you in danger, though. You have to know that I need to protect you from a different level too."

It was my turn to give him a nod as our waitress approached and clocked the change we made to the table. I could see the minute she decided it wasn't her business. I wasn't prepared for why she decided that, though.

"Travis, do I even want to know why you decided to rearrange our furniture?"

My pseudo-date turned and glanced up at the new blonde waitress. I didn't see the woman who had seated us anywhere, which was strange. This one had incredibly perky boobs and more cleavage on display than should be allowed during the lunchtime, family-friendly rush. She leaned in and took advantage of his position to plant a red lipsticked kiss on his cheek. If I didn't know any better, I would have sworn she had gone in for a full lip lock, but he turned away just enough before she got there that her mark was left on his cheek near the corner of his mouth instead.

"Mindy, what the fuck are you doing?" he asked as he leaned back, which put him closer to me. I silently handed him my white cloth napkin. He took it, noticed where my eyes tracked to, and then proceeded to wipe away the lipstick Mindy left behind.

"What? I can't greet an old lover?" she asked as her eyes drifted my way to get my reaction. The woman wouldn't get one. I didn't play desperate bitch games.

"I'll take a water with lemon and no ice, though we already ordered our drinks from our waitress who seated us."

Mindy's eyes narrowed on me momentarily before she turned her attention back to my date. "What about you, sugar?"

"I'll take the water I ordered from Jessica after she's sent back to our table."

"What?" Mindy gasped. "Why?" Her eyes darted around, as if she were looking to make sure no one heard that last bit.

Bigfoot leaned in closer. "You damn well know that you don't ever attempt to put a claim on a club member, especially in public and when he's obviously on a date, unless he gave you his property patch."

She huffed and waved his words off. "Come on, we both know she's not your date." The woman looked me over again and was obviously unimpressed by what she saw. The roll of her eyes told me as much before she turned her full attention back to Bigfoot. "We both know she isn't even close to being your type."

She probably wasn't wrong there. His son's mother was a platinum blonde. Mindy was not far off. They were both surgically enhanced in places where I was lucky to fit into a C-cup during the time in my cycle when my bra size inflated just a little bit. The only makeup I had on was mascara and the little bit of tinted lip balm. That was more to keep my lips from drying out than about looking good. Mindy, on the other hand, had clearly gone heavy with the contouring to make her nose appear smaller and jawline stand out more.

Bigfoot stood then and glared down at the woman before he looked up and yelled, "Where is the fucking manager? Is Jennika here?"

"Please," Mindy cried out as she grabbed my date's arm and pleaded with him. I would worry about the fact that I acknowledged him as my date later - when he didn't have another woman throwing herself at him. "Don't do this. I will get Jessica to come back over and cover your table."

He snatched her hand off his arm and offered her a menacing grin that should have made her quake in her insensible shoes. "You had your chance to do that, and you chose to come out here and pull your shit, then to stick around and piss me off some more."

"We have a history," she whispered, though her desperate attempt to connect with him in a way that might create a sympathetic response ended up making it more of a whiny plea. It also made things worse for her.

"We fucked a few times, years ago, and I haven't touched

you since then. All we have is a history that wasn't worth remembering in the first place. I don't know why you thought I would react any other way to you disrespecting my date. That's something I never did for you, by the way, take you on a date. But just in case you missed the fucking memo, you were never important to me, and I will never put up with someone disrespecting my woman."

"I'm sorry," She repeated as she backed away. The manager finally made his way over to us and glanced worriedly between Bigfoot and Mindy before he sighed.

"Mindy, get your things, clock out, and head home."

"No. Johnny, I need the money."

"You should have thought about that before you made our guests angry."

"I'm not angry," I told him. "I am thirsty though."

"Apologies," the man insisted. "I'll have Jessica bring your drinks right away." He turned and grabbed Mindy's arm, since she still hadn't moved. As he rushed our second waitress away, I heard him ask her where Jessica was and what the fuck she was thinking by pulling that shit with the one man who had the power to run them all out of town.

"Sammy, I'm so sorry about that. I swear, there is nothing going on with her."

I rolled my eyes and returned my attention to the menu. "Obviously. She was testing the waters for some reason, but that isn't my problem. Beyond making sure it doesn't happen again; it isn't yours either."

He chuckled such a deep, rich sound that it sent a little tingle of awareness up my spine. I glanced back up and saw the sparkle of humor in his eyes. "You are not like any woman I have ever known."

My attention flitted to where Mindy and the manager had disappeared into the kitchen. "I'll take that as a compliment."

"As you should." He chuckled again as he offered up his agreement. "Seriously, she doesn't mean shit to me. I've barely spoken more than a few words to her in the past couple years. There was a brief time when..."

I cut him off before he started to spill details I didn't want. "Look, we all have a past. I get it. You're a bit older than me, so you have more of a past than I do. I'm not asking for details, a list of women who you've fucked, had relationships with, or anything else. You have already assured me that you are not married, in a relationship, or fucking around with anyone else right now. Unless any of those things have changed, you have nothing to disclose."

"Okay," he said as he took a minute to look over the menu as well. "Nothing has changed unless you count the fact that I want to be in a relationship with you."

I smirked before my eyes lifted to meet his. "That wasn't subtle at all."

"Wasn't trying to be."

"I'll let you know," I teased.

"Christ! I should have known you were going to be a fuck of a lot of work."

"You know where the door is, since we both have a decent view of it."

He squeezed my hand and I noticed in my peripheral that he also shook his head. "Not a chance, Sammy. You're going to be all mine. You just haven't caught up with the program yet."

A minute later, our waters made their way to the table

and our original waitress was back with apologies and looking a little worse for the wear. "I'm so sorry. That whore locked me in the damn bathroom. Can you believe it?"

"After what she just pulled, I have little doubt," I said to her. "No need to apologize."

"I can't believe she did that. Mindy has never been subtle, but that was over the top, even for her."

"It won't happen again," Bigfoot announced.

"No, it won't because she was fired, and I don't think there is a place in town who will hire her after word gets around."

"She could always go work for Marisol's Manor in the back rooms," I suggested.

"I think fucking not," Bigfoot said as he glared down at me. Maybe it was my suggestion that earned the glare. Either way, I shrugged it off. "That's a club-owned business, and she won't find work with us."

I slid my menu over to Jessica. "I'll take the Tomato Bisque and grilled cheese, please." Our waitress nodded and turned her attention to Bigfoot.

"J's burger, fries, and I want the chili on it."

"Be back shortly," Jessica said before she scurried away as quickly as possible.

"Did you not know we owned both bars in town?"

"I knew. I just figured it wouldn't matter if she was working there."

"Why would you think I'd allow a woman who disrespected both of us to work at any establishment owned by my club?"

I glanced around the diner and then back to Bigfoot. "Honestly, there aren't a whole lot of women around here that might earn you guys some money in your establishment. I figured you might make an exception to keep the place staffed for paying customers."

"Jesus, woman. You are something else. Don't worry about the talent, the guys will go find women and bring them here to work if we run out of options."

"And that scouting mission will be totally above board and their choice?" I questioned, because as much as I knew about the club, there were also the rumors that ran rampant around town. Some of those rumors involved the club running women against their will. I wasn't certain I believed that, but it was better to get the question out of the way before it became a little thread of worry that I picked at later.

"Always their choice, baby. We may not be legit in all the ways, but we don't traffic people. That's a hard line. If they're not willing, they don't work for us. If they change their mind at any point, we send them on their way with enough cash to start fresh somewhere else."

"Good to know."

"Anything else you need to know about my club?"

"Nope." I stared into his eyes to let him know that I meant that. It was the only thing that worried me about the club. Anything else was just extra stuff. I didn't care about the guns or drugs, or whatever else people claimed they did. It was obvious that the men of the club and the people of Violence didn't have a drug problem. That told me more about how they kept their business away from home than words and promises ever could.

"Okay then, let's backtrack a minute."

"To when?" I asked.

"Earlier, the way Jess wished you luck with me."

That was a weird thought to pick back up on, so I waited for him to provide the clarity that he obviously needed to share. "Jess is Melissa's best friend." I must have given him my best blank stare, because he felt the need to add. "Melissa is Hawk's mom."

"Right." I felt like a moron for not putting that together. I had heard both of them call her Lis up to that point.

"Anyway, do you really think she would have said that to you if I was with Melissa?"

"Listen, I already told you that I believed you two weren't an item."

"Then what's the problem with us making an official go of this thing between us?"

"The problem is that she felt comfortable enough to try to chase me away to begin with. There's also the fact that she used your son as an excuse to do it. I don't want to cause problems with your son. I also know what it's like to hate a stepparent with all my heart. I wasn't around when my dad started to date his wife, but I would never want a kid to feel for me the way I feel about Colleen. It caused a major rift between my father and me, and that was before I knew she truly didn't care if I lived or died."

"It wouldn't be like that," Bigfoot tried to assure me.

"Wouldn't it? If your ex really didn't want me around, don't you think that would cause notable issues with your son? She's his mom, whether she's in the right or not, Hawk will take her feelings into consideration, and it will have an impact on the way he sees me. I don't want to be the enemy coming between you and your son or the cordial dynamic you've had with his mom up until now."

When Bigfoot remained quiet and contemplative as our

food was delivered, I knew I had to break the ice again. I didn't like the fact that he was stuck in his head. "Besides, how am I supposed to know if you're not really a fuck buddy with your boy's mom? I mean, if you think about it, this could be some weird game you guys play. You pick up an extra woman here and there to spice up your bedroom life. For your information, I am not down for a threesome with your ex."

Our waitress chose that moment to return to the table to check on us and nearly spilled a jug of water as she guffawed at my last statement. "Oh lord, I don't know if I'll make it through this shift if I keep overhearing bits and pieces of your conversation."

"Keep it to yourself," Bigfoot ordered her. "Sammy's being a bit of a brat today."

"Looks like you enjoy her bratty side."

"Jessica!" Her name was a warning, albeit a playful one.

Our waitress threw her hands up in the air and chuckled as she moved away from us. "I'm going and my lips are sealed."

Once she was gone, Bigfoot grabbed my hand and pulled it onto this thigh as he held tight. "I told you before that I don't share and I sure as fuck won't be shared either. That means not with another man, woman, or anyone who finds themselves anywhere between the two."

"What about the guy who has two dicks? I've always wondered about that one. Does it make him a double man or..."

"Sammy." The exasperated way Bigfoot said my name made me laugh.

"Kidding," I managed to get out before I whispered, "kind of." I mean, who hasn't wondered about that?

"You keep right on playing hard to get with me, baby, but there's no need. I'm already hard and definitely out to get you. Only you."

"Oh!" Well, that left me speechless and a little tingly in places that weren't appropriate to speak of during the lunch rush at Jennika's family-friendly diner.

15. FAMILY MATTERS

BIGFOOT

I did not want to leave Sammy in the care of Kingston again, especially since he was still an untried prospect, but I didn't have much of a choice. That meant that I had to trust more in Sammy's ability to take care of herself than I did in the fact that I had a man watching her back. As we walked back to the library, Glitch sent me a message that we needed to meet up because he had new information that we all needed to see.

I hadn't been back in the clubhouse more than two minutes when he came around the corner and hitched his thumb back toward the office. "We're all waiting," Glitch threw out before he turned back around and hauled ass in that direction. I didn't take offense to a club member ordering me around. I knew he didn't mean shit by it. Glitch fit his name. There was something his brain that didn't connect with other humans. That was fine because what didn't work with human interaction sure the fuck worked wonders when he had a keyboard at his fingertips.

"I take it you found something important that might

help with our current situation?" I asked the minute the office door closed behind me.

Glitch nodded as Baffle made his way to my side. "Found a link between the Mojave Devils MC, The Rivera Cartel, and the man in town they have on their payroll." I knew before he even confirmed who it would be.

"Sheriff Estes?" I questioned.

"That would be the one. Not sure if either of his two deputies are on the take with him, not that it would matter. If it came down to it, I don't think he'd have an issue getting rid of them."

I turned from Glitch to my VP. "Do we know what the fuck is so special about Violence that the Rivera Cartel would buy off our sheriff? We aren't close enough to the border with Mexico to matter to them."

"Seems someone thinks that there is a mineable resource between Fox Mountain and Black Peak that will produce some precious minerals and resources the Cartel wants possession of. Our club property and the town of Violence is the closest settlement to those would-be mines."

"They want to turn Violence into their own personal mining town?" I asked, unable to believe the bullshit I was hearing. "There are wind turbines between us and the mountains. It's not fucking feasible."

"It's possible my source is a little off the mark. Cerro La Mula isn't far from us either. It's also not part of the Apache National Forest, so they won't have the issues with mining there that they would near the other mountains. Plus, you know what we found here on our property."

I turned to Baffle and understood immediately. The caves beneath our property hadn't simply yielded a great place for our grow farm, they had also granted us an unexpected mining operation of our own. There was a healthy load of gold, copper, and zinc beneath our feet. It was how we managed to obtain more property as it became available. It was also how we funded our businesses in an area where there hadn't been much development previously. The town of Violence sprung up around our club, not the other way around.

"We are not going to let the fucking cartel or the damn Mojave Devils move in on our town."

"No, we're not," Baffle agreed. "We need to redirect their attention somewhere else. We might be able to fight off the MDMC, but the Rivera Cartel has a longer reach and more resources. I'm not sure how we'd fare against them if push came to shove."

"Luckily, I think they've only been putting out feelers and haven't fully committed yet," Glitch informed us.

"They tried to kill me, in case we all forgot how this shit happened." I pointed to my not yet healed arm. "Do you seriously think this has all been a push to get fucking mineral rights or easier access to them?"

"It's our best guess so far, and considering what we found in our own backyard, it's not improbable. All they would have needed was for some idiot to find something in his backyard or on a hiking trip, and then for him to run his mouth about what he found and where. Whoever that fucker was that tipped them off is probably dead somewhere while they've been searching for signs that he wasn't fucking lying." Baffle turned and paced to the other side of the office and back again. "Why does it feel like we're missing something?"

Someone banged on the office door, and I moved to open it. "What's going on?"

"Sorry to interrupt, Prez. There are some men out at the gate requesting to see you."

"Did you get a name or at the very least a description of the men, Prospect?"

His face turned red as he nodded his head. "Yeah, sorry. They're the Morton brothers that run that campground."

"Have them sent up and bring them directly back to my office."

Once the prospect was gone, I turned back to my club brothers. "This can't be a good sign."

"Maybe they're tired of you stalking their girl," Knuckles grinned like an idiot as he said it.

"That's the other piece of the puzzle we need to figure out," Baffle reminded me.

"What do you mean?"

His eyes drifted back to Glitch before they returned to me, and he spoke again. "There has to be a reason a woman affiliated with the Mojave Devils ended up married to Brian fucking Morton. And if my suspicions are confirmed, then this takeover of our town has been in the works for a long fucking time. We're spinning our wheels playing catch up until we get the full picture."

A knock sounded on the door a few minutes later as we all sat there quietly contemplating what Baffle had just laid at our feet. I opened the door, and before the prospect could announce the Morton men, they stormed into my office. Brian was caught up short when he realized I hadn't been alone.

"We need to talk," he finally said.

"Then talk."

Brian glanced around and seemed nervous to speak in front of the men in the room with him. I wasn't going to have him waste my fucking time though, not when we were fucking hip-deep in a takeover we thought was only ankle-deep a few minutes prior.

"These are all my club's officers. I don't have secrets from them, so whatever you have to say, you need to fucking say it now or don't. We don't have time for you to stand around and contemplate life while you wait for me to empty out my office for you, though. That shit ain't happening."

Brady seemed amused. Josh, the middle brother, appeared to be along for the ride. Brian grew angry and finally decided to say what was on his mind.

"You need to stay the fuck away from my daughter."

"That so?" I asked.

"Yeah, that's so. She doesn't need to get involved with your MC or any trouble you have brewing. She's a good girl and has been through enough without adding your band of thugs to the mix."

"Thugs? Really, Bri?" Brady asked his oldest brother.

"What would you call them?"

"Allies, if you're smart," Brady explained. I grinned at him and then turned my focus back to the man who didn't seem to care much about his own daughter before he walked into my office.

"It's too late to keep Sammy away from club business. It's already at her doorstep. I'm already there, and I don't plan on walking away from her. She saved my life, and if there wasn't another reason, that would be enough to keep her under our protection."

"So, this is a favor for a favor thing?" Brian asked. I had already started to shake my head, but he ignored the gesture and carried on. "If you want to do my little girl a favor, you will forget about her. Leave her alone to live her life without all the bullshit the club will bring into it." His chest heaved with the effort to speak passionately about his need for us to leave his daughter alone.

"Does your vehement dislike of our club around your daughter have anything to do with your wife?" Baffle asked.

"My wife? What the fuck does my wife have to do with anything?" I glanced from Brian to Brady and then Baffle before turning back to Brian to answer his question.

"She has been linked to a rival club of ours. The Mojave Devils," I tacked on to see if their name sparked a response from him. The man seemed clueless.

"No. She's not involved with an MC. She's a stay-at-home mom, for Christ's sake."

I glanced back at Brady who looked disappointed in his brother. "She's been keeping secrets from you, Bri."

"What the fuck is that supposed to mean? What secrets?"

Brady explained to his brothers, after a healthy warning from me about keeping shit to themselves, what happened with the Devil Sammy killed and how he had been sent to her cabin by Colleen Morton.

"That can't be," Brian denied.

"I have the security video. You obviously never told your wife about the cameras. Maybe there was a reason for that. I think somewhere deep down you knew you couldn't trust her the way you pretended to." Brady didn't wait for his brother to accept or deny that claim. Instead, he pulled out his phone and shoved it in his brother's face. "Watch. That's your wife, gleefully showing a biker where to find your daughter so he can kill her."

"She wouldn't do that," Brian denied again. "You don't know that's why she sent him there."

Brady took his phone back and pulled something else up. "That is your daughter's mattress. Those three holes are from the three rounds that fucker put into her bed, thinking she was sleeping in it. If she hadn't heard something that woke her up, she would have been dead. Instead, she killed the fucker. The fact is your wife sent him there. Whether she ordered the hit or just pointed him in Sammy's direction, Colleen knew he didn't have good intentions toward her."

The middle brother appeared stunned and remained silent until Brian turned on him. "Did you fucking know about Colleen? Is that why you were so fucking determined that I get my daughter away from the club? You're the reason we're here today. You swore Sammy would be in danger if we allowed them to keep tailing her everywhere. Are you in on this shit - whatever it is - with Colleen?"

"Fuck you if you think I'd ever harm my niece for that cunt you married. You're the one who brought that bitch into our lives because you were too fucking busy thinking with your dick and running wild after Joy died to think about wrapping your cock up."

"Then why? Why were you so damn hard up to keep my daughter away from the Kings of Anarchy?" That was something I was curious to have answered as well. I thought them being here was Brian's doing, not the middle brother who Sammy barely even talked about.

Josh scrubbed his hands down his face as he shook his head back and forth slowly. Then, instead of addressing his brother, he turned his attention fully on me. "Fuck!" he spat out. "I'm sorry man."

"What the fuck have you done?" Immediately, I thought maybe he got into bed with the MDMC or the Cartel, but what he ended up admitting to was something I never would have seen coming in a million years.

"She told me to do whatever it took, so things wouldn't get complicated."

"Who told you? What the fuck did this bitch say to make you want to keep Sammy away from me?"

"I've been dating Melissa for almost a year," he admitted. I was blown away and so were my club brothers from the looks of all the shocked faces in the room. "We've kept it quiet, but when she realized who Sammy was at the hospital, she called me immediately and said there was no way we could allow that shit to happen. If you hooked up with Sammy, you would demand that Melissa couldn't be with me."

"What the fuck?"

"That's what she said."

"Why the fuck would I do that?" I asked him. "I don't give two fucking shits who Lis dates as long as they treat my boy right if it's serious between them."

Josh laughed and then looked down at his feet as he admitted her reasoning. "Because it would look pretty fucking incestuous for me to be your son's stepfather one day while my niece becomes his stepmom."

My eyes widened as I glanced around the room to get my brothers's take on that revelation. We were all shocked for approximately two minutes before I burst out laughing right along with Baffle and Knuckles. Glitch stood there with his arms crossed over his chest and his eyes focused on Josh and Brian.

"That's actually pretty funny," I admitted. "You'd be Uncle Daddy and Sammy would be Mommy Cousin." I laughed louder as the words left me because it sounded even more ridiculous out loud than it did in my own head. The Morton brothers stared at me like I'd lost my mind. Well, two of them did that. Brady's shoulders shook as he laughed along with me.

"I wish Sammy had been here to hear that," Brady eventually admitted.

"That's my daughter! Are you telling me you're not just protecting her because she saved you, but that you're interested in her romantically? Does she know that?"

"I am and she does."

"And did she agree to date you?"

I laughed again as all the times Sammy had denied me flashed through my mind. "Right now, she thinks I'm stalking her, but eventually I'll wear her down," I joked just to get a rise out of Brian.

"What the fuck did you just say?"

"Fucking relax, asshole. I'm only half kidding. Melissa, who happens to be my son's mother and your brother's secret girlfriend, gave your daughter the impression that we were very much together as a couple when she met her in the hospital." I turned my attention from Brian to Josh then. "Good luck explaining to your niece how you've been dating Lis for a year when it was Lis who told her that she's my ol' lady."

"Son of a bitch!" Josh growled. "She doesn't know how to make life easy on a man, does she?"

There was a reason I'd never even considered getting serious with Melissa, even after she found out she was pregnant. In fact, I fully believed her pregnancy had been a goal of hers, because she thought it would force my hand. She learned quickly that shit was not going to go her way.

"Nope," I finally answered Josh. "Why do you think I never made her my ol' lady when she had my kid?" I chuckled at the contemplative look on his face. "She's not my biggest concern right now, though I'll deal with her bullshit later." I turned back to Brian. "Your ol' lady is my problem, and we need to deal with her because there's no telling what the fuck she's been up to or what she has put in the works."

"The house!" Brady shouted. "Colleen has been adamant about getting our parents' home, but Dad left it to Sammy."

"What's the point?" Josh asked.

"The point is that I moved Sammy into the house after that incident with the fucking Mojave Devil. She said that it looked like someone had been cleaning things out of the house that shouldn't have been taken and moved some things in that shouldn't be there." He turned to his brothers then. "The grandfather clock is one of the pieces missing." There was something important in that statement, but Brian spoke before I could ask questions.

"She's been on me to get Sammy to sign something giving us the house. She probably thought I'd get it done and started to redecorate."

"Why the fuck would she think that? You know damn well Sam was planning to renovate before she moved in. We already got the master bath done and were about to start working on the kitchen. She wouldn't renovate just to give up her claim on the house."

"She's been living in the cabin, I figured I could talk her around, since I have a kid that needs more space." That statement worked to piss Brady right the fuck off.

"Funny that space was plenty big enough for you to raise Sammy with Joy but not enough to raise Ryan with Colleen," Brady spat at him.

"Shut the fuck up!" I yelled out to silence the brothers who devolved into a whole name-calling situation after that.

"Brady, why are you concerned about what Colleen has taken out of or put in the house?"

"Besides the fact that the clock was a priceless piece of our family history dating back to 1740s Scotland, and belonged to Sammy?" he questioned, then I watched as the blood drained from his face. "What if she had the place wired up?" he eventually asked.

"Wired up..." I repeated as the words sank in. "Fuck. Glitch!"

"On it, boss." He turned to the Morton brothers. "One of you needs to come with me, so I can't be accused of trespassing. Not that I'd care, but I can't help Sammy if your bitch wife decides to call the law on me." Glitch threw a pointed look back toward me. He couldn't mention to the civilians that our local sheriff was dirty and working for the people trying to kill Sammy and me. They were close to the situation, but not close enough that we could share that, considering we weren't really sure how Brian would react or what he might pass back to his wife - whether intentionally or not.

"Brady and Brian stay. We have things to discuss. You go," I said as I pointed my finger at Josh. "We'll figure shit out later where the family dynamics are concerned." Josh nodded and followed behind Glitch as they got ready to leave the office. I stopped him with one question, because it was important that I got the answer to it before he hauled ass. "Are you serious about Melissa?"

"Yeah, I am."

"Even though she claimed me as her old man in front of your niece?"

Josh heaved out a somewhat defeated sigh. "She panicked. I'm not fucking happy about it, but it's something we can work through."

"All right. You handle Lis. I'll handle Sammy."

"No one is handling my daughter," Brian insisted.

"Shut up!" Josh and I said at the same time. Josh grinned at me before he added his own threat - if you could call it that. "You better treat her right. She's still my niece, and you fuck with her, or she gets hurt, I don't give a damn that you have a club at your back. I will find a spot for you inside the fucking mountain and make sure your sorry carcass is never found. You feel me?"

"I feel you. Same goes for my boy. Don't give a rat's ass about his mom aside from her being whole and healthy for my son's sake, but you fuck things up for him, and you won't even make it inside a mountain. I'll leave you as carrion for the creatures in the desert." He nodded his head and left with Glitch to go check on my woman's house.

16. OFF THE RADAR

SAMMY

I WASN'T SURE WHAT WAS GOING ON WITH THE CLUB, BUT BIGFOOT hadn't been my shadow for a few days. In fact, the last time I'd seen him was three days earlier when he dropped me back off at the library after our weird lunch at the diner. It felt almost as if my family had been avoiding me too.

My dad was a given, since he didn't pay me much attention when his wife was around anyway. Josh had been strange for weeks, so it was par for the course with whatever he was going through. The bigger issue was that Uncle Brady hadn't dropped by like he normally did. I would have been concerned, but he did at least text me and finally called last night to tell me he had to go out of town to search for some parts for a motorcycle.

That left me in the company of the club's prospect, Kingston, who felt more like a ghost lurking about than anything else. I tried to invite him into the house, and you would have thought I threatened to cut his balls off with a dull butter knife.

Eventually, the poor kid had to do more than just piss.

That was the one time he asked to come inside, and it was also when I took the opportunity to give him the slip. I hoped like hell I hadn't just ruined his chances at becoming a club member, but I needed to get to Albuquerque to take an exam, and there was no way I could do that with a very conspicuous shadow following me around. I was lucky enough to be one of the few students who were granted a spot in the remote student program with the Anderson School of Management. While it was part of the University of New Mexico, they normally had a pretty stringent "must attend in person" policy. The only thing I wasn't exempt from attending in person was my exams.

My school was a little over a two-hour drive away. Considering my shadow wouldn't take two hours to shit in my bathroom, I turned my phone off for the drive there. Once I got to the school, I left it off since I'd be sitting for a test and didn't want to be accused of cheating or get thrown out because my phone went off in the middle of the exam.

I knew that it was risky but hoped that whoever had been targeting the Kings of Anarchy MC realized that I wasn't a soft target after two of their men disappeared. Then again, I supposed that could backfire on me since they'd be out for revenge for their friends. Those were the thoughts that threatened to cripple my ability to do well on the exam. Every time I had to think too hard to come up with an answer, a random thought of enemies lurking in the background would pop into my head. It made me want to search the room for anyone paying too close attention to me, but I had to refrain. Me glancing around at all the other students in the exam wouldn't look good.

It might not have been a terrible thing to have the

prospect shadow me to school, unfortunately it was too late to consider that option. Once I finally finished with the exam and turned it in, I reached into my bag and turned my phone on and was instantly greeted by a text from Bigfoot.

Bigfoot: You can't hide from me Sammy. I'm coming for you. You're mine!

Sammy: You're the hide and seek champ, not me. "Me Bigfoot. Me come for you. Blah, blah, blah!"

Bigfoot: You'll come for me baby. That'll be the best part.

Sammy: 😔

Bigfoot: Prospect is already on his way to Albuquerque, baby. You should have known better than to slip away from club protection. He was there to be your shield, should it be necessary.

Sammy: I had an exam and they don't exactly let you have a buddy sit with you when you take them.

Bigfoot: You could have mentioned it, and we would have worked something out.

Sammy: I guess I'll know for next time.

I hated that he was being so civil about my disobedience, especially since I knew how seriously he took my safety. It made me equal parts swoony and hot to think about the way the man cared for me, and then there was his text about making me cum. It was probably a good thing he wasn't there. We might have ended up in the slammer for public indecency, to hell with his baggage and my issues.

Bigfoot: Which part of campus are you on?

I was about to answer when I heard the scrape of someone's shoe too close to me for comfort. I glanced up to see two goons dressed in suits approaching from either side of me. At first, I thought maybe they were feds or some sort of law enforcement who came to try to get me to inform on the Kings of Anarchy, but that wasn't the case. When I looked a little closer, it became obvious that they were both Hispanic, and the suits were nothing like what feds might wear. These were designer garments, and the men did not have that polished and put together look that went with the clothing they wore. They looked more like soldiers playing dress-up.

Despite the fact that the parking lot was still crowded, the two goons quickly pushed me into the back of what looked like an armored Range Rover. That was no easy feat. I might have been tall for a woman, but the vehicle had been lifted and one of the goons had to shove me up and into the seat. Once I was able to sit upright, I came face-to-face with a man who identified himself as Diego Rivera.

"Do you know who I am?" he asked. I didn't bother to answer more than to simply shake my head. He sighed. "Seems the further we get from the border, the less known we are. It is both a blessing and a curse."

"I'd truly love to sit here and feed your ego until you feel good about who you are again and your place in the world, but I'd much rather you get to whatever other point there was in kidnapping me."

He chuckled lightly and his eyes sparkled with the genuine humor he found in my words. "A woman who doesn't have a healthy sense of fear, I see." He nodded as if answering his own unasked question. "It makes sense, since it is reported that you may have taken out two of the men who work for my family."

"I don't know what you're talking about," I insisted.

"Of course you don't. Not intelligent enough to keep from being a smart-mouth but aware enough to deny killing my men." He smiled and tapped the seat between us with his finger. While I was focused on that, he leaned forward. "Let me be more clear then, shall I?" When I didn't answer, he continued. "A man went missing on a night when you were the only person in his vicinity who wasn't too injured to do anything to him. It was a quiet stretch of US-60 just over the border into New Mexico from Arizona."

"Contrary to popular belief, I am not some sort of guardian angel of US-60. It was fate that I was even on the road when a man crashed. How am I also expected to be there when someone else crashes or goes missing?"

"There you go again with that smart mouth." It was obvious that he was more amused than annoyed with me, but I knew if I kept it up, I would run his patience dry. "I have it on good authority that he was there at the time of the crash, and that you would have seen him there."

"The only thing I saw was a truck blow a tire, a man on a

motorcycle go down, and then I called for help for him. Literally, that was everything that happened that night, and then I followed the man to the hospital because I've never seen someone wreck like that, and it fucked with my head a bit. I still have nightmares," I admitted truthfully.

"And the man who came to your house never to be seen again?" he questioned. "Did you also not see him?"

"Oh no, I killed that fucker when he pulled a gun on me in my own home."

Diego seemed startled by my quick admission. "If that was the case, then why haven't the cops heard about this supposed home invasion, or found his body?"

"Fuck the cops!" I spat out. "I'm not trying to go to prison for life because some dumb fuck thought I was an easy target for whatever fucked-up games you boys play with one another. I'm not a member of any club, cartel, organization, or whatever. I fucking work at a campground, go to school - as you know - and I mind my own fucking business. I'm about sick of all this bullshit falling in my lap for no good reason."

The man seemed to contemplate my heated words for a moment and then he glanced around and took notice of people who had their phones aimed at his vehicle. He nodded and then turned back to me. "We never had this conversation." He then leaned across me, opened my door, and shoved me out. I stumbled and fell on my ass as his man came forward and shut the door before the Land Rover took off. The two goons glared down at me as my cell phone rang in my pocket. Then, they took off toward another SUV and hopped in. Once they were out of sight, a couple of the people who had been standing around filming, came over and helped me up.

"Thanks," I muttered.

"That was so scary. I thought you were never going to be seen again!" One of the girls cried out.

"I called the cops," another admitted. Great. That was something I didn't need to happen.

"You can call them back and tell them I'm fine."

"They shoved you into an SUV and then threw you back out. How is that fine?" The girl asked. My phone started to ring again and that time I reached back and pulled it out of my back pocket. I was lucky that it hadn't been damaged when I tumbled to my ass.

"What the fuck, Sammy?"

"Sorry, two men threw me into the back of a Range Rover with a man named Diego Rivera."

"Mother fucker!" Bigfoot yelled down the line.

I quickly explained what happened and that my nosy fellow students probably saved my life. That or my use of humor to cope with shitty situations. "I think he was amused by me," I told Bigfoot. He growled at me in response and my belly fluttered with nerves that had hidden themselves while I was in the middle of my own kidnapping story. "Seriously," I attempted to reassure him. "There were a fuck ton of people with cameras pointed in our direction because class just let out and they saw me being pushed into a car against my will."

"Stay put. Kingston and another club brother will be there to escort you home. Do not leave without my club there to see you back safely. I mean it, Sammy." I could hear the anger in his voice, but worse than that was the worry."

"Are you coming?" I asked after a minute.

"No. My son was hurt at school, and I'm on my way to the hospital with him."

"What are you doing on the phone with me then?"

"Making sure you are safe and okay because I can't be in two fucking places at once."

"Sorry, you should go. Your focus should be on Hawk. He's your priority and I'm literally no one to you."

"You're very wrong about that, Sammy. I'll prove it to you later, but for now you need to remember you are very important to me, too. When my brothers show up to escort you home, they are going to bring you to the clubhouse and you are not going to fight them on that."

"Okay."

"Good." He hung up after that, and I felt like complete shit. This man was trying to keep me safe and despite my best intentions, I managed to pull his focus off his son at a crucial time anyway. If I had just been a big girl about things, we could have worked out having an escort with me while I took my exam. He was right about that. Beyond that, I was finally frightened about my situation. Diego Rivera, despite me saying otherwise, was widely known as the right-hand man of the Rivera Cartel. They were brothers. Emiliano was the boss, but Diego and Alejandro - his younger brothers - were next in line for the throne if anything happened to him. I had been in Diego's vehicle, and I wasn't completely stupid. He didn't let me go simply because a few cell phones were pointed in his direction. I didn't think he even cared about them.

The fact that I didn't know why he hadn't taken me with him was scarier than anything else because it also meant that he could show back up at any time. I think that was what he wanted, for me to be set free but to know I was still his captive anyway. He had taken me from the middle of a busy parking lot, which meant he could take me from anywhere.

17. SHROOM AND DOOM

BIGFOOT

I WALKED INTO MY CLUBHOUSE WITH MY SON IN MY ARMS. HE WAS knocked out from the pain meds the doc had given him when he set and casted my boy's arm. Thankfully, it was a clean break that didn't require surgery of any kind. Still, my boy had been miserable before they finally gave him meds to manage the pain.

My eyes darted around the wide expanse of our club-house until they landed on my woman. She scared the abso-lute shit out of me when she pulled her disappearing act. Then, to find out she had been in the hands of Diego Rivera made me almost leave my son in the care of my men. Diego was the brother known for heading up the human trafficking side of the Rivera Cartel business. He was a ruthless fucker who didn't hesitate to take out his enemies. If what Sammy said was true and she humored him, that was almost a scarier proposition than not getting her home. It made me wonder why he set her free and what that meant for her future. Protecting her from the Mojave Devil's MC was one thing. Protecting her from an obsessed Diego Rivera would be a whole different level.

I moved closer and deposited Hawk on the couch closest to me, so I could go wrap my woman in my arms and reassure myself that she was there, safe inside the walls of my clubhouse. When I got closer, it finally hit me who Sammy was sitting with. Rosalie was on one side of her and Sweatpea and Princess were on the other.

"They've been regaling her with stories about which brother fucks the best and how you rank." I turned to see Baffle beside me with an amused look on his face.

"Why the fuck did you let that happen?" How in the hell had my woman made friends with the club girls? That shit never happened. Ol' ladies never mixed with the free-range pussy on tap for any of the brothers to use. It did not give me a good feeling.

"Do you still not know the woman you claimed? There's no letting Sammy do something, she just does."

"Fuck's sake!" I grumbled. "Sammy!" I called out to her. When she turned to find me, the grin that spread across her face told me I was in big trouble. I just didn't know if I would enjoy it or end up hearing a never-ending litany of reasons why we couldn't be together. First it was Melissa, then it would be the women who hung around the club to give it up to the brothers.

"I should have made sure Kingston put her in my suite," I said under my breath.

Baffle laughed, slapped me on my back, and wished me luck before he moved back over to the bar.

"How is Hawk? Is he going to be okay?" Sammy said by

way of greeting. I smiled down at her, thankful that my boy was the first thing on her mind.

"It was a clean break. He has a cast for the next six weeks or so. The doctor thinks it will heal up just fine as long as we can keep him from injuring himself again." Sammy chuckled at that.

"Boys will be boys and all that?" she asked.

"Something like that."

"To be expected, considering who his father is," she added.

"I need to get him tucked into bed. Come upstairs with me?" I made it a question, but there was no way I could leave her down here now that I laid eyes on her. "Need you with me," I said before she could respond.

"Okay, I'll follow you."

I was thankful as fuck that we wouldn't have to have a private conversation amidst the whole fucking club and the few hangers-on who lingered about. "I'll have a talk with the club girls about what's appropriate and not afterward. That should have never happened."

"No. You're not going to do that. I asked them a question and they answered me in the most respectful way possible. They didn't volunteer any information that wasn't requested, and I'm not holding what they said against you. We weren't together when you slept with them, right?"

"Fuck, Sam. I didn't sleep with all of them."

She winked at me. "I know. They told me. Rosalie was the only one." She winked at me playfully. "At least of the three who would talk to me anyway. Some of the other girls wouldn't come near me as soon as they heard my name."

"They're the smart ones." Sammy laughed at my

response. "Can you grab my keys out of my front, right pocket. The long, silver one opens my door."

Sammy reached into my pants pocket and I had to try very hard not to pop a fucking boner considering I had my boy in my arms. It felt good to have her fingers on me, even if she was innocently reaching for my keys. Once she got my door opened and we walked inside, I heard Sammy gasp.

"Wow. I was not expecting this!" I turned and smiled at her. "You were expecting some shithole with posters of naked women lining the walls?"

"Well, yeah," she admitted. I watched for a minute as she spun and took the whole place in - at least what she could see of it.

"Second door on the left, can you make sure it's open?" I asked. I still wasn't all the way healed from my accident and carrying Hawk was taking a toll on my fucking body. My arm shook and the one that had been broken - much like my son's - screamed at me for the strain I put it under.

"Oh my God!" Sammy all but shouted. "You shouldn't be carrying him like that."

"He doesn't weigh that much," I argued as I got him to his bedroom and laid him down on top of the covers. I bent to pull his shoes off and ended up sucking in a hard breath as pain shot up through my ribs and straight into my chest. It felt like something inside ripped all over again, and I cursed myself for not getting Baffle or one of the other men to bring my son up to my rooms for me.

"Here, let me do that," Sammy offered as she gently pushed me out of the way and bent to take my boy's shoes off his feet.

"Do you think he'll be out for a while?" Sammy asked as she lifted a fleece blanket up over my boy and tucked him in.

"They gave him some pretty strong meds." I held my hand out to her. "Come on, let's go to the other room to talk."

When we made our way back to the living room, Sammy looked around in awe again. "Honestly, this is amazing. I always thought you guys only had like one room and a shared bathroom for like twelve of you."

"That's pretty specific," I teased.

"It may have been a fantasy at some point."

"To fuck twelve of my club brothers?" I couldn't even name twelve of the bastards who would be fit to breathe the same air as her, let alone fuck her.

She giggled. "No, but there were these fantasies I had based on a television show and being a fly on the wall in the shower when you all came in to get clean."

"You think we throw communal shower parties?" I groaned. "Fuck's sake, no wonder you didn't want anything to do with me. You thought I'd been here having sausage fest showers."

She giggled again, and it pleased me to notice that she kept her laughter contained so as not to disturb my boy. "Stop trying to make me laugh. Tell me about Hawk. Is he really going to be okay, and where is Melissa?"

I shook my head. "We'll get to that in a minute. You scared the fuck out of me today."

"Honestly?" she questioned. "I scared the hell out of myself too. What if he hadn't let me go?" She curled up next to me and let her head droop down to rest on my shoulder on my uninjured side. "He could have taken me. I don't know why he didn't, but that's all I keep thinking about. My life as I know it could be over."

"Maybe, for tonight, we should just thank our lucky fucking stars that he let you out of that vehicle and leave it at that. I'm not sure I can handle a conversation about one of the biggest human traffickers in our area having had you so close when there was nothing I could have done to save you."

I stood from the couch, where we had tucked in only a moment ago. "Come on, I need something different right now."

"Something like?" Sammy asked.

"Something like you in my arms with very few clothes between us."

"What's going on here?"

"What do you think is going on? I already told you exactly what I want. You're mine, Sammy. My ol' lady, if you'll have me. My only woman, and I want to be your only man. It's as simple as that. I won't share you and I'd never ask you to share me. It's just the two of us in this."

"And your son, his mom, your club, my family…"

I shook my head. "Nope. They all matter to us, but they don't have a say in what's happening between us. That is a you and me zone."

A smile spread on her face. "I kind of like that. A you and me zone."

"Good because I meant it. Haven't been with another woman since before my accident and don't plan to again now that I have you."

"How can you be so sure? It hasn't been that long since we met."

"Three weeks and five days," I told her.

Her eyes widened, as did her smile. "You're counting how long we've known one another?"

"I may have been keeping track of how long it took to get you to agree that you're mine." I leaned down and kissed the tip of her nose. "I want you because you're different. You can handle your shit. You don't panic. You take action. You're fucking loyal as hell, even when you have no reason to be other than your curiosity or conscience or whatever got the best of you. It kept you by my side in the hospital."

"Maybe that was loyalty, or perhaps it was because of the fantasies I was having about you. Maybe, I didn't want to give them up so soon."

"Whatever kept you there, I'm thankful as fuck for it."

We walked into my bedroom and stood there for a minute before I took matters into my own hands. I pulled my cut off and laid it gently on the back of my desk chair. Then I reached over and pulled her shirt free from her body. She didn't try to stop me and that only encouraged me to keep going. By the time I had her down to her bra and panties and me in my boxer briefs, I moved us closer to the bed.

"I feel like you're forgetting a few key pieces of clothing there, big guy."

"We still have some things to talk about first before I take those last pieces off."

"That sounds ominous."

"I hope it's not."

"Well, you better spill it then because I'm not really good with the whole anticipation thing."

I opened my mouth to tell her when someone started to frantically beat on the door. I jumped up and ran over to the door to keep whoever it was from waking Hawk. "What the fuck is so urgent?"

"We need you in the lower level now." Baffle wasn't usually one to lose his cool, but his tone suggested there was a big fucking emergency. Lower level was their code word for the cave system.

"What the hell is going on that you need me down there?"

"The shit we found before is spreading." Dime said. "What you did before should have kept it from spreading, but..."

"Give me a minute to get some clothes on and figure something out. I'll be right down."

I shut the door in their faces and went back to the bedroom where I immediately caught Sammy's eyes. She looked like a fucking angel there in my bed. I hated the fact that I was the president for the first time in my life. "I'm about to trust you with something important. No one outside of this room is to know that you were made aware."

"You have my word."

With anyone else it wouldn't have been enough, but I trusted Sammy. "We have a problem in our grow house?"

She snickered. "Your pot not producing to standard?"

"Not pot, baby. We grow shrooms in the cave system below ground."

"You grow what now?"

I pushed my hand through the longer hair on top of my head and sighed as my eyes met hers again. "Shrooms."

"The kind that get people all fucked up and seeing shit that isn't there?" She asked.

"Yeah, baby."

I waited for her judgement, but it never came. Instead she sat there on her knees in my bed in nothing but a purple bra and panty set that had my mouth watering. "What's the problem?"

"Something funky is happening to them and we need to try to salvage what we can. I have to go and..." Hawk came to mind. "Shit, I need to call my mom to come get Hawk."

"Or you can go take care of business and I can stay here for when he wakes up. Does he need meds again or food or..." She cut herself off and I knew in that moment that I wasn't just claiming her. I would make it official and marry her too. The woman put me, my kid, and my club above everything else, despite the day she had.

"Loyal to a fucking fault," I muttered.

"What?"

"Nothing. He's good for meds. I'll be back before he needs more. His discharge papers and everything are in the bag over there on my desk. Are you sure you want to do this?"

"Of course." She climbed out of the bed and grabbed my t-shirt up off the floor. When she dragged it over her head and let it settle, it hung down almost to her knees. "Go, take care of business and maybe call Uncle Josh to help you."

"Josh?" I asked.

She grinned. "He's a horticulture expert. He has a fancy degree he never tells anyone about, but he also grows a lot of shit. He's the one who takes care of the food we grow as a co-op endeavor at the campground. We're all supposed to pitch in, but most of it falls on Josh since he has the green thumb in the family and not many of the campers stick around long enough to reap the benefits, so they don't bother with putting in the effort."

"Good to know. I'll give him a call. Thanks, baby. My phone is on me, in case Hawk has any trouble." I knew for a fact that Josh was out of town with Melissa. It was the reason I had to be the one to get to the hospital to be there for our son. He needed at least one of his parents there with him.

"We'll be just fine."

I leaned in and kissed the hell out of her before I turned and left to go try to salvage whatever was left of our fucking crop.

18. THE MOMSTER

SAMMY

Since I was in Bigfoot's rooms alone with his kid, I took the time to get dressed again instead of waiting to see if he showed up in time to have the rest of our conversation and then maybe seal the deal on our relationship. His son's comfort, should he wake up and find his dad missing, was my number one priority.

As I waited, my phone sounded a text notification. At first, I thought it was Bigfoot checking in, but that was a little ridiculous since he had only just left. Then again, he had told me about their grow house but not where it was located. It was possible he needed to fill me in on that little detail.

When I finally pulled it out and glanced down, it was to see what looked like an angry text from my dad.

> Dad: Where is Colleen?

> Sammy: How the hell should I know?

Dad: Because I'm betting money that your biker boyfriend took her.

Sammy: I seriously have no clue, but I'll find out if that's true as soon as I can.

I stewed in my questions for what felt like an hour before I finally broke down and texted Bigfoot.

Sammy: Are you almost done? Everything okay?

I hated to be that person, but what if he made up the shroom excuse to go torture Colleen for being a bitch? I thought about that for a minute and two things jumped out at me. The first was that "an emergency with a shroom grow operation" seemed like a weird lie to tell. The second was that I wasn't exactly mad at the prospect of someone putting Colleen in her place - even with physical violence - considering the fact that she stole my inheritance and was still actively trying to steal the rest of it out from under me. Fuck her all the way to hell and back.

I was lost in a weird stream of hate-fueled fantasies of offing my dad's wife when the door to the room burst open.

"Is Hawk okay? Are you? What's going on?"

"We're fine."

"You texted me."

"Yes, because I was curious how long it would take to get some answers I need."

"About what?"

"Well, my dad texted me and he swore that you might have kidnapped my stepmonster." Bigfoot looked angry and it made me wonder. "You did, didn't you?" I questioned.

"The thing I wanted to tell you before we were interrupted?" he said, though it sounded more like a question. I gestured for him to get on with it. "Well, we've been looking into your stepmom, and we were ready to pounce on her the minute she tried to skip town."

"Where is she?"

"I don't fucking know because I got called to handle Hawk, the guys left to get you, and I'm guessing she used that opportunity somehow to slip through our surveillance."

"Why did you have her under surveillance, other than she's a giant twat who should have choked on her own umbilical cord before disgracing the Earth with her birth?"

"That was vivid," he said as I shrugged. It was true as far as I was concerned.

"We know that she told the second assassin where to find you." I sat still and listened, so Bigfoot carried on. "Then we realized that there was more to her story. Glitch dug up some information that led us to believe she has loyal family ties to the Mojave Devils MC." I nodded, still waiting for the part of all this that would surprise me. "When your dad and uncles told us about the furniture being tampered with in the house you inherited and moved into recently, it made us wonder if she tampered with anything else. I had Glitch check to see if the place was bugged."

"Was it?"

Bigfoot nodded. "I guarantee it's how they knew you were headed to school for an exam today. We got the bugs, but not before they knew your plans. Since you didn't share them with us and slipped your tail, we had no way of knowing where you would be. It proves the MDMC is involved somehow with the Rivera Cartel, though."

"You think Colleen set me up to give herself time to break away because she suspected we were on to her?" I asked.

"Seems likely considering your father texted thinking we took her."

"That bitch. I hope she fell into a giant fire ant pit, naked, and that they eat her alive. Except for her diseased cunt because I don't think even fire ants would touch that."

"Again, vivid. Your dad..."

"Eww, please don't say what I think you're going to say."

Bigfoot threw his head back and laughed. "Ah, no, that was not where I was going to go with that."

"Wait! What about my brother?" I asked as I grabbed my phone and dialed my dad's number. It only took two rings before he answered. "Sammy?"

"Dad, where is Ryan? Did she take him with her?"

"Of course she didn't. Your man took her, and they left Ryan behind. He's the one who told me that the man put her on the back of his motorcycle and left with her."

"Dad, Bigfoot didn't take Colleen."

"Don't lie for him. Or hell, maybe he's lying to you. It's obvious it was him after our conversation earlier."

"I promise you that it wasn't him."

"I don't believe you." Bigfoot took my cell from me and put it on speaker, so my dad could hear him too. "We do not have Colleen. If we were going to take the bitch, it sure as fuck wouldn't be on the back of one of our bikes."

"Why the hell not?"

"That's a sacred space meant for our women only, Brian. Your daughter, as my ol' lady, will be the only woman to ride behind me unless we have a daughter of our own one day. Then she can ride there too. Not all clubs honor that tradition, but our chapter of the Kings of Anarchy does. No one rides with us unless they plan to be together for life."

"Then who in the hell rode off with my wife?"

"My guess would be one of the Mojave Devils."

"Check with Brady. He can pull the security camera footage," I suggested. Bigfoot pulled out his phone and texted someone. As he was doing that, Dad started to cry into the phone.

"I need help, Sammy. You need to come home and help me with Ryan. He's beside himself because his mom left him here alone. I don't know what to do to calm him down, and I think... I think there are things missing that I need to check on."

Bigfoot looked up from his phone and shook his head. "That's not going to happen, Brian. Sammy isn't safe on your property right now. If you want her help, you can come to the clubhouse with your boy, and she can help if she chooses to. Her safety comes first, and that is something I will not compromise on."

"How is she not safe at home with her family?" Dad asked.

"You left your wife in charge of the campground for days. There is a camper who checked in during that time. An assassin put three rounds in your daughter's bed, and she was forced to do something about that. There are cameras planted in her home. They were watching her and all of that was done right under your nose. Sammy will be here where my club can keep her safe. That shit is not up for further discussion."

AN HOUR LATER, my dad showed up with Ryan and informed us that Colleen had cleaned out their joint checking and savings accounts. "She also took copies of the family trust paperwork." That caught Bigfoot's attention, and he hopped back on his phone.

"Baffle, need Doc here with some DNA test kits." He listened for a minute and hung up. "We need to test you and Ryan to see if he's your son."

"What the fuck do you mean? Fuck you. Of course, he's my son."

I shook my head. "You never had a test done. You believed her and we know she's a lying bitch."

"She wouldn't leave her own son behind with me if he wasn't mine."

"We really don't know what she would do at this point, Dad."

"I know you're pissed, but you're going to have to hang on to that anger for a little while. If Ryan was your son, then he would stand to inherit the entire family trust if something happened to all of you." As Bigfoot explained, Colleen's plan became crystal clear in my mind.

I turned to my dad and took hold of his hands. "It means they kill all of us and they can use Ryan to take control of the land."

Dad folded in on himself and made a horrible noise that held equal notes of regret and frustration. "How could I have had a fucking monster living with me all this time? I married that woman."

"We need to get Uncle Brady and Josh here, now," I told Bigfoot. He nodded his agreement.

"Fair warning, that means Lis will be coming in too, since she's with Josh."

"What?"

"That was the other thing I needed to tell you earlier," he admitted. "The real reason she lied to you is because she's been seeing Josh in secret for a year. They didn't think any of us would be able to deal with the family dynamic it would create if we were a couple too. So, she wanted to make sure that you wouldn't be interested in me."

"What family dynamic?" I asked. Bigfoot smirked and then laid it out for me. "As your Uncle Josh put it, he would be Hawk's Uncle-Stepdaddy and you would become his Cousin-Stepmom."

It was so ridiculous that I burst out laughing. "Oh my God, that's kind of hilarious." I continued to laugh and some of the people around me joined in. "Why do the Morton men all have really shitty taste in women, though?" I asked. My dad winced, but I wasn't sorry for saying it. He had ruined our relationship for a woman whose whole goal was to have a baby with him, kill us all off, and steal our land.

"Why would she leave her son behind, if he was the key to obtaining the land?"

"That's why I want Doc to run their DNA."

He didn't think Ryan was my dad's son. Unfortunately, I had come to the same conclusion.

19. CROWDED HOUSE
BIGFOOT

S<small>AMMY WAS OFF ON ONE SIDE OF THE CLUBHOUSE PLAYING A GAME</small> with her brother and my son. The boys were only about a year apart in age and, thankfully, got along well. I was trying to do some online research about what might be wrong with our mushrooms, but I if there was one thing I sucked at worse than growing the fucking things, it was research.

"Have I mentioned lately how fucking much it sucks that Twitch went on that ski trip and ended up dead?" I growled.

"There has to be someone who knows something about mushrooms." Baffle was just as exhausted as I was. We had been pulled in several different directions all at once non-stop lately and it was getting old and wearing us all down fast.

"Why do you need to know about mushrooms?"

I turned to see Sammy's Uncle Josh standing there.

"You guys made good time getting back," I announced to change the subject.

"Yeah, not playing around with Lis's safety, and if I'm in

danger because I'm a Morton, that puts her in danger by being with me."

I nodded my head. If he'd put his woman ahead of himself like that, then there was hope for them and for me not killing him for being an asshole stepfather to my son.

"So, what was it you needed to know about mushrooms?"

"Say you have a bunch of mushrooms growing in an enclosed space, and a batch of them has either a weird web-like substance growing around them or there's a fine powdery substance and the fuckers are starting to turn pink and brown in spots. What do you think that could be?"

"Sounds like Cobweb Disease, but I'd have to see it to know for sure."

"Cobweb Disease?" Baffle asked. "That's a real thing?"

"You can look it up." Josh nodded to the phone in my hand. I did just that and turned my phone to show Baffle a picture that looked a lot like what was going on with our shrooms.

"You need to come with me," I ordered as I stood up. "And keep in mind that this shit does not get back to Lis. If I find out she knows, it will be your ass on the line."

"Whatever you say, Bigfoot," Josh tossed out on a defeated sounding sigh.

"Anything else, we'll come to a compromise on. This is club business and I'm trusting you with it solely based on your connection to my woman."

"Melissa isn't your woman!" he growled it out like the threat it was meant to be.

I laughed at him. "Nope, she sure the fuck is not. Your niece, however, is my woman."

"Since when?" Josh asked.

"Since the moment she saved my bacon on the side of the road."

"Dammit, Lis is not going to like that shit."

"Don't really give a damn what she likes. She can get over it."

As soon as we got Josh downstairs and he saw what I did, he grinned. "Looks like you already took the right steps. Airtight isolation until you can get this shit cleaned out. Be sure you don't unseal the plastic until you have this whole section cleaned properly though, the spores, or whatever the fuck they are linger on everything."

"The problem is that the next section looks to be infected too. It was just a little behind this one, so we didn't notice the webbing in the soil."

"Damn. Let me through to see, then. We'll see what we can salvage and how much needs to be culled."

"There's no saving them once they're infected?"

"Nope. As you have learned, the shit spreads fairly easily, especially in an enclosed space where the powdery shit has nowhere to blow but to the next section. Every time someone walked by one section to the next, some of that powder probably went with them either on the smallest breeze kicked up by walking by, or it may have clung to their clothing."

"How the hell do we even get something like this down here?" I asked.

"Someone might have brought it in from the outside."

"Sabotage?"

"I didn't say that." Josh was quick to point out. "It could have been as innocent as walking by an infected mushroom.

Some of the powder might have been trapped on clothing, in hair, or on someone's shoes when they came down here, just enough shook loose that it was able to start infecting the mushrooms you have growing. I don't know who your grower is, but they should have known and been able to catch this quickly."

"Our genius behind this operation took a ski trip and got himself killed. We thought we could handle growing them ourselves, but obviously there are things we weren't aware of that are causing a major setback now."

"I'll see what I can do to salvage some of your crop down here. Do you have more of the plastic?"

"We do. I'll send our guy down that helped me with it last time. He can show you where everything is."

I LEFT Josh downstairs to deal with our shroom problem and made my way back up to confer with my VP. "Think it's time to let Big Daddy in on the bullshit we have going down?"

"Yeah, put in a call to him. I talked to Rio, since he's Prez of the West Texas Chapter, and they've been having their own issues with the assholes."

"When did you do that?"

"While you were taking care of Hawk. They believe the Mojave Devils are trying to expand into their territory to aid the cartel too, but I don't think they're after the land for the same reasons there. They're not aware of any precious mineral deposits on the land. We think it's more about getting rid of the competition."

As soon as I got in touch, Big Daddy assured me he would put the rest of the clubs on notice about the Mojave Devils and the Rivera Cartel. It was the best I could do for the other chapters while I worried about what was going on inside my own.

When I got back to the main gathering area in the clubhouse, all I wanted to do was wrap my woman up in my arms, check on Hawk, maybe grab some food, and then take a fucking nap. Unfortunately for me, that shit was not in the cards. The minute I stepped foot in the common area, my eyes tracked straight to Sammy and in doing so, Melissa as well. She was running her mouth to my woman, and I wasn't having that shit. I double-timed it across the space and stepped between the women.

"What kind of shit are you lying about now, Lis?" I may have said that a little too loudly.

Sammy tugged on my arm and shook her head once then used her eyes to tell me quietly that there were little ears who heard me. Dammit.

"I swear to you, Travis, I was just telling Sammy that I was sorry for being mean to her when we met in the hospital. It was a mistake on my part, and she already knows why."

"Mom was keeping secrets about her boyfriend," Hawk said to me.

"Is that so, little man?"

"Yeah, she told me to keep it a secret too." His lip poked out and wobbled a bit. "I didn't want to lie. I'm sorry, Dad. You don't hate me, do you?"

"Never, buddy. I could never hate you." I glared up at Lis,

though. "We'll discuss that later," I promised her. I'd be damned if she was going to train my boy to lie to me and make him feel like shit for it.

"Sorry," she whispered.

"Not good enough," I muttered as I held my son to me. "Why don't you go play with Ryan while he's still hanging out with us?"

"Okay. I'm not in trouble?"

"Not this time. No more lying to me, though. Lies are what get people hurt and in trouble."

"Yes, sir," my boy said, and then, because he was smarter than I was at his age, he took off like lightning across the room toward his new friend.

"Why don't you go take a load off, big guy. You look worn out." I leaned down and kissed Sammy on the forehead.

"My parents are here," I said as I clocked them coming in the clubhouse.

"Go say hi. I'll be over here for a minute. Melissa and I weren't done with our conversation before you interrupted and I was just about to tell her the secret to handling Uncle Josh." That surprised me. It really had looked like Lis had been giving my woman a mouthful of attitude, but I supposed it could look the same as her bitching about her man doing something she didn't like.

I gave my mom a hug, but she didn't stick around to speak with me. Instead, she bee-lined for her grandson and wrapped him up in a big hug. I smiled as my dad ambled up to my side. "That your new woman over there with your son's mom?"

"It is."

"Looks a little intense," he mentioned as he snagged a beer from behind the counter.

"I just learned my lesson not to get involved. Sammy can handle herself."

"Son, I have no doubt because there's no way you'd ever land yourself a weak woman."

"Hey, Crutch, welcome back!" Baffle called out as he made his way over to us.

"Hear you boys have been busy," my dad said.

"Too busy of late."

"So I hear. Now tell me what the fuck's been going on with the club that Punchy had to call me and give me a head's up that we might be going into lockdown."

"Fucking Punchy," I groused. The man was once the VP of the club when my dad was president. Whereas Crutch was all too eager to give it up and hand over the gavel to the next generation, Punchy had not been. Dad had my mom as the driving force on his retirement. I don't think Punchy liked his ol' lady much anymore, if he ever did.

After I filled my dad in on everything, including the update we got from Josh that we might need to harvest the crop sooner than later if we planned to have anything we could sell, Crutch offered up a clever suggestion.

"How's about Punchy, me, and a couple younger members or prospects take the product to our distributors. We can make it sound like the older generation is out there training the baby bikers to ride better. The law ain't gonna look to the old guys and non-patched as potential targets or mules. We can get the product out on time while you deal with all the other bullshit going on."

"Sounds like a solid plan," Baffle agreed with him. "It would free up some of our time to get other shit in order."

Dad winked at me and then grinned at something over my shoulder. "Your mom might kill me for going, so we might have to sacrifice your new woman to her. Keep her from thinking about the risks I'll be taking."

"You don't have to do this."

"Ah, fuck that son. This is still my club. I'm still a member. I ain't fucking slacking on my duties just because I don't wear that President's patch anymore."

"Fine. You're the one who has to tell mom, though."

He shook his head. "I was thinking you could pass that information along after we leave."

I laughed at the old man. "Coward. I'm not doing your dirty work for you."

"See if I ever volunteer to do you a favor again," he said as he walked over to where my mom was talking to Sammy while they watched the boys play.

"You not going with him for backup?" Baffle asked.

"Fuck, no. I'm not stupid. I won't get within distance of her throwing arm when he tells her he's going on a club run."

Baffle laughed. I didn't. My mom was capable of a lot of shit, especially when she was pissed off. Her vacation with my dad to see friends in Montana had already been cut short thanks to Hawk's accident. She wasn't going to be happy when she discovered my dad was going to head off without her for a bit.

"Looks like your woman might be smoothing shit over for both of you. Crutch looks like he just fell under Sammy's spell, too."

I chuckled. "I don't know if I should wait of the other shoe to drop or thank my fucking lucky stars that they're all getting along."

"The kids are glued to the TV, Trav. You should probably let Lis look after them while you go save your woman from being the referee for your parents. Maybe sneak off and make sure to thank her lucky stars as you create them."

Finally getting Sammy beneath me sounded like the best plan anyone had presented me with in recent months. I wasn't going to say no to the opportunity. "Make sure they know that the boys need looking after once we're clear," I told my best friend.

"I got your back," he said as I took off and tugged my woman away from my family.

20. AWKWARD
SAMMY

"Travis Blane Cardwell, don't think I don't know what you just did there." I heard Tilly call out as Bigfoot dragged me away from his parents.

"Mom's mad, we have to go quick." I laughed as he increased his pace and dragged me along behind him. "I'd pick you up and carry you, but we're still a couple weeks away from me being able to do that. You're going to have to fend for yourself a little bit longer."

"Your mom was telling me what it would be like to be an ol' lady."

"Oh yeah? I can't imagine she told you how good all the orgasms would be."

"Eww, why would she tell me that?"

"She wouldn't, but that's the perk I have to offer and it's better than anything my mom could have told you."

I laughed at him again. "You're an idiot."

"Yeah, that might be so, but Sammy, I'm your fucking idiot for as long as you'll have me."

"I'm tired of fighting this thing between us. Hawk

doesn't seem to hold it against me that I was the stranger in the hospital with you. I think I have my brother to thank for that, though. He helped break the ice between us."

"That's good."

"It is because it's important. Your parents seemed lovely, even though I'm a little concerned for your dad's safety at the moment."

"He'll be fine." Bigfoot chuckled as he unlocked the door and tugged me into his room. "Now, let's leave all that bullshit out there because," He turned to lock the door behind us, "this is our space in here right now. We both need a break from the constant family and club bullshit that keeps hitting us from every side. What do you say we strip down again and take that nap we planned on earlier?"

"Aww, I forgot you're an old man. See, earlier, I thought we were stripping down to do what naked people do under the covers." I winked at him as I tugged my shirt up over my head. "Here's a hint, it has nothing to do with sleeping."

Our clothes disappeared before I could even blink. "I'll show you what my age really means."

"That you're going to only be able to get it up once?" I teased.

"Fuck that, you're going to see how different it is to be with someone who knows what the fuck they're doing."

"So, you're telling me that 24-year-old Bigfoot was a minute man with no skill?"

"Keep taunting me brat," he said as he yanked my panties off and smacked my ass.

"If you promise to keep spanking me like that, I might continue to be a brat."

He smacked my ass again and then grabbed a handful as

he growled into my ear. "Baby, be glad I don't have full use of two hands right now. You'd be red as a cherry right here," he explained as he gripped my ass cheek harder.

"I guess we'll have something to look forward to when you heal. Now, tell me what's going to work best for you because I know those ribs aren't all the way healed up yet."

"As much as I want to throw you down on your hands and knees and take you hard right now, I think it might be best if you ride me instead."

"I can do that," I teased him as I leaned down and placed the tiniest whisper of a kiss on his cock head. "Now, get your ass on that bed and get comfortable."

"Yes ma'am."

One of the reasons I was so drawn to Bigfoot was his overbearing demeanor. I wanted him to take charge of me, toss me around, and fuck me stupid. That was the fantasy. The reality with him still recuperating was a little bit different. It was a challenge, and I wanted to rise to the occasion and make the most of it for both of us.

After he got into position, comfortably relaxed against a stack of pillows propped up by his headboard, I slowly made my way up his body. I started at his ankles - because feet were gross, especially fresh out of a biker's boots. "Your mom three-naming you was the first time I knew your full name," I said that in between kissing my way up his thighs.

"All you had to do was ask, baby."

"How old are you?"

"I'm thirty-four, but you already knew that, since I went to school with Brady."

"I knew you were around there. You could have been held back a year or started late or something."

"Baby, I really want you to get to know as much about me as you want, but can we postpone the getting to know you conversation until after we both get an orgasm?"

I nipped his balls and he shrieked like a little girl, then it changed to a moan as I sucked them into my mouth. That shut him up. I ran my fingers up the trail of brown hair that went from his cock to his navel. "I love that you don't shave this off. It's sexy as fuck."

"Yeah, baby?" he asked as he scooped my hair up and held it in place behind my neck. I leaned in and sucked his cock to the back of my throat and made a noise, "Mmmhmmm," to tell him that yes, that was right. "Fuck, Sammy. That's so good. Do it again." I hummed and sucked him all the way to the back of my throat again. It was lucky that I didn't have a gag reflex to get in the way.

"Holy shit, baby. As much as I want to feel your pussy wrapped around me, I can't imagine losing that mouth of yours to do it."

I nipped the tip of his cock in a playful, not painful way. "Shh, I'm trying to concentrate," I said before I bobbed back down on his dick. Travis pulled my hair and twisted it tight, then used the hold to guide my head up and down. On each downward motion, I sucked him in hard. Whenever he pulled back, I licked my way up his length, and teased him as I blew cool air on top of the warm wetness left behind by my mouth.

"Fuck yeah, that's amazing, baby."

"Not near as amazing as it's going to feel when I ride you like you've never been ridden before." That might have come off a little cockier than I intended, but when Travis's cock twitched against my lips, I knew he enjoyed hearing it.

He tapped my shoulder with his weak hand while his strong one still had my hair bunched up at the nape of my neck. "Climb up here, baby. I don't want to cum in your mouth."

"I'm on the patch," I told him.

"Patch?" he asked and seemed confused by that.

"Birth control patch," I told him and turned ever so slightly so he could see the patch that was stuck to my shoulder blade.

"I didn't even know that was a thing. I'm clean. Had myself tested before they discharged me from the hospital."

"That was very intuitive of you."

"I like to think ahead." He patted his thighs. "Now, hop up here because I have it on good authority that someone is going to ride me like I've never been ridden before."

"Oh yeah, maybe I should call Rosalie up here," I teased.

Travis smacked my ass, and the sting made me close my eyes and throw my head back. "That's exactly how I want you to look when you have my cock in you, now get up here."

I did as he asked. Travis held his cock steady, and I slid onto it at a painfully slow pace. "Fuck, woman, you're killing me."

"I'm savoring this feeling. We only get one first time."

"Fuck that. We get as many firsts as we want with one another because it's all new between us."

"I like that."

"Good, now fucking ride me like your life depends on it."

And I did.

21. INTERROGATIONS
BIGFOOT

Everyone except the old-timers and younger members who went on the run to deliver the mushrooms to our buyers had been on lockdown for nearly a week, and we were all getting pretty sick of one another's faces. I loved my club brothers and their families, but there was a reason we opted for a compound where we had individual houses built, too. The problem was that we had grown beyond those houses. We needed more land to be able to house everyone within our fenced property, while also keeping people from being crowded on top of one another and the clubhouse.

We also had extra bodies with Sammy's family under our roof, too. I couldn't complain about that either, since Josh had saved our asses and our future crops. Had we let the disease spread much further, we would have lost the whole business and not known how to start it back up. Since we lost our one and only mushroom guru before, I put Josh in charge of teaching some of the guys how to care for our crop and what to look out for in the future. We also established clean room rules for anyone who went down into the cave. It was imperative for us not to introduce shit we might pick up from outside to our underground farm.

"Doc has the DNA results. He's on his way here now," I announced when Brian finally joined us all downstairs. His face drained of color at the mention of the DNA test and then he sat down and shoved his face into his hands. I could tell by the slump of his shoulders that he already suspected what Sammy and I had figured out. Ryan wasn't his.

"What the hell am I supposed to do if he's not mine?" Brian asked the room at large. My mom and Lis had the boys in the gaming room upstairs, so we weren't in danger of them overhearing us. "What the fuck am I supposed to tell that boy about his mom? Why didn't I ask for a test before? Fuck!"

"She preyed on a heartbroken man, and you let her because you needed to move on from Mom. You can't regret anything if Ryan really is yours. You just have to try to figure out how to tell him about his mom in a way he will understand, because there is no coming back from this for her. Her intention was to kill all of us off, since the trust was finally explained to her, and she knew that was the only way to get it." Sammy explained to her dad.

"Yeah, that works if he's mine. What if he's not? What am I supposed to do?"

"He's been your son since before he was born, Dad. You have held him, bathed him, told him stories, and taught him the things you know. You signed his birth certificate. It's the same as if you had willingly adopted a child. You don't give them back just because you realized they weren't going to look like you. He's yours. He's ours. That little boy will forever be my brother because it isn't fair to take our family away from him, when his only crime is having a cunt for a mother."

Brian nodded his head, and I gave my woman a little squeeze. She was the best of the best. Loyalty dripped from her veins and there was nothing fucking sexier to me than that.

I glanced around to make sure there were no lurkers to overhear when I told Sammy and her dad that we located Colleen. "She's shacked up with good ol' Sheriff Estes."

"Fuck. You think he's the father?" Brian asked. My woman smacked him on the arm. "What did I just say? No matter the results of that test, you are still his dad. So, stop asking yourself who he came from biologically, because he belongs to our hearts."

"You're right. It's just, what if he knows and he tries to fight us for him?"

"That won't happen," I assured him.

"How can you be so sure?"

"Because Estes isn't long for this world. He was in on the second assassination attempt against Sammy. No man threatens my woman's life and lives." I stood and walked away from them to let what I had to say seep in and for them to come to terms with it. I didn't think Sammy would have a problem with how I just put shit, but Brian was made of softer stuff than his daughter and brothers were. The more time I was forced to spend with him, the more it became obvious. The way Sammy and the other Mortons talked about him, the more I thought his spirit did pass on with his first wife. He sounded like someone I would have liked when

Joy Cosay was still alive. Once she passed to the next world, a part of him did, as well.

WE WORKED over Estes for two fucking hours and the bastard was either a champion under pressure or he didn't know shit about shit. He was simply on the Riveras' payroll, but obviously wasn't a key player. I was sure Colleen knew more, but the men were loath to torture another woman.

"How about we use Sammy to do it?" Knuckles asked. He earned a brand-new shiner as a result. "What? Come on, Prez. It's not like she hasn't killed for you before. Besides, this bitch tried to off her entire family, or at least planned to do so. I'm pretty sure your woman would want a few minutes alone with her."

"That might be, but I don't like the idea of my woman being used."

"Then offer her the choice," Baffle interjected. "If she says no, then we figure something out. If she wants to do it, we let her."

"Yeah? And which of you will be there for her when she wakes at night from nightmares about what she had to do to get information for us?"

Dime snickered. "No offense man, but I don't think your woman will be wallowing in nightmares. When it comes to the wet work, she seems to have a switch she can flip and disassociate what's going down around her. Love that for her."

"Fuck. Okay," I agreed because Dime wasn't wrong. It was something I'd spent time marveling over as well.

Knuckles, Baffle, Glitch, and I made our way back upstairs while Dime stayed put with our prisoners. As soon as we got upstairs, it was like Sammy had some kind of radar. She homed in on me and then got up and made her way to our little huddle.

"What's going on?"

"Come with us first," I told her. She followed all of us down into the secret caves beneath the compound.

"This is cool."

"We need to ask you something." Glitch got right to the point while ignoring how Sammy felt about where we were.

"So, ask."

"We need a woman to coerce the information we need from Colleen."

"Why do you think I'd be able to do it?" I could tell by her demeanor that Sammy was fucking with him, but as per usual with Glitch, he didn't catch on right away.

"You were in the Army. Didn't they teach you interrogation techniques?"

"I was in the Army, not the fucking C.I.A." She laughed as she corrected him.

"So, they didn't teach you anything?"

"I was a Quartermaster, Glitch."

"What's that mean?"

"It could mean a lot of things that involve being support staff for the troops, but for me, it meant that I packed parachutes."

"You packed..." Glitch's brows pulled together as he tried

to fit Sammy into that field of work. She laughed at him again.

"You've clearly been watching too many contrived Hollywood movies, Glitchy-poo. I packed parachutes. I didn't off people. I didn't interrogate anyone. I didn't even fire a weapon except during training and quals."

"She's always been a useless little bitch!" Colleen yelled from the chair she had been secured to. Sammy strolled over and smacked her across the face. "I'm sorry, what was that? I couldn't hear you around the shit that was coming out of your mouth."

"I said you are a useless bitch!" the woman growled at her. Sammy grabbed her by the hair and yanked her head back so fast, Colleen let out a startled yelp. While she was disoriented from the quick movement, she hadn't seen Sammy pick up a knife from the table of materials that had been left there to intimidate the bitch into talking. Sammy didn't care about appearances. She was pissed and stabbed the knife into Colleen's thigh just an inch from where her groin was.

Colleen screamed.

"I didn't fucking hear you," Sammy whispered into her ear. "Now, you were saying something about who you were working for."

"My Uncle. Hammer. He-he-he needed someone to get close to one of the Mortons. I tried with Josh when he was drunk, but he didn't even give me a sideways glance and then, thankfully, didn't remember me when Brian introduced us later."

"Why the fuck were you supposed to get close to my family?"

"Your family is nothing. We need your land."

"You could have killed us all off."

Colleen shook her head violently. "No. If we didn't have a legal right to take it, and killed all of you, the trust states that the land is donated to the state and is to remain open to the public's use."

"So, you set out to baby trap one of the Morton boys?" she asked.

"I had to."

"No, you really fucking didn't." Sammy took another knife and stabbed Colleen's other thigh.

"Why?" Colleen screamed. Sammy laughed at her. "I'm telling you things..."

"That was just because you're a bitch and I didn't like what you were telling me. Now, I suggest you answer whatever questions these men have for you, or I'm going to get creative with the pieces of you I start to carve up next, Colleen." As if to emphasize where she might start, Sammy took a third knife and tapped against the woman's pussy.

I looked at Sammy then turned to Baffle. "Get what you need. If she gives you a hard time, call me and I'll bring Sammy back to deal with her."

"Where are you going?"

"To fuck my woman." I grabbed my cock and adjusted it. "Fuck, I'm so hard right now, I can't stand it." I grabbed Sammy up, threw her over my shoulder and ignored the pain that ripped down my side. It was nothing compared to a few weeks ago. Technically, I was healed up. That didn't mean everything wasn't still tender when I put it under strain. I made my way down the long hall before I finally kicked a door open and went inside. It ended up being an oversized supply closet. It would have to do.

"Can't wait to get you upstairs, baby."

"Good," she said as I set her back down on her feet.

I smirked when the heat in her eyes made it obvious she was in the same state I was."Now, strip for me, baby, because I need to fuck you hard."

22. NOT THE FATHER

SAMMY

Doc never showed up when he said he would with the DNA results, but it was for good reason. He was called to help another chapter out with an injured man. I wasn't sure what everyone hid from me about that call, but there was a reason the club member couldn't be taken to the hospital and it had nothing to do with someone reporting a gunshot or stab wound to the police. From what I'd gathered, there was something about the blood work coming back with disturbing results. I shook it off because it was none of my fucking business and truthfully, I shouldn't have been anywhere near that conversation. I had gone to ask Bigfoot if I could go with Grease and Forge to help shut down the businesses on my family's land. As it turned out, there were a few squatters who had pulled their RVs into the campground and made themselves at home.

When Bigfoot told me that I couldn't go, I put in a call to Jake.

"Hey, long time no hear from you," Jake said when he picked up.

"Yeah, well, I got caught up in some stuff and had to take a little vacation."

"Oh, that's good. I thought you were avoiding me because of the disaster date."

"You owe me for that bullshit. If you thought she was cheating on you, you could have at least clued me in before I got there. I would have had fun with it instead of ditching you with them to go home and not wash my hair."

Jake chuckled at that. "I guess that's fair. I could have been honest with you, but then I would have had to be honest with myself. Suspecting and coming to terms with it are two different things. I still hoped that I was wrong when we went to meet up with them that night."

"Okay, well, I was calling to tell you that there are a couple Kings of Anarchy MC members who are coming to shut down all the businesses for us. It's temporary and we'll still pay your base wages while we're shut down."

"What's going on, Sam?"

"No need to worry, just do me a solid and make sure they get everything turned off and properly shut down and locked up at both garages before you go. They're going to have their hands full kicking out the campers who decided to squat there when we hadn't been seen on the property for a few days. And Jake," I added at the last minute.

"Yeah?"

"If they run into any trouble while they're there, I want you to hide and call me immediately. Okay?"

"You want me to hide from trouble like a little bitch?"

"Yes, because having eyes on a problem is better than having a dead employee who can't help give information to us if it becomes necessary."

"Damn. You sound like you're part of a special ops team and I'm helping you out on the sly."

"Something like that. Just promise me that you'll stay safe if something pops off."

"I promise. I'll find a good hidey-hole and call you or Brady."

"Okay, good. Talk soon." I hung up before Jake could ask any other questions. He already knew too much as far as I was concerned.

"Doc's on his way in," Bigfoot told me as he leaned in and kissed my cheek.

"For real this time?"

"For real, I promise. He's about five minutes out, so you might want to have your dad and uncles meet us in my office. Tell him to leave his kid with Tilly. She's out in the common room."

No sooner did everyone congregate in Bigfoot's office than Doc came through the doors with an envelope in hand. "Sorry for the delay. Shit was crazy..." When Doc realized there were several civilians in the room, he quickly shut his mouth.

"We'll discuss that shit later. Right now, we need to know if the kid is Brian's or not."

Doc slid a finger under the sealed envelope and ripped it open. He slipped the papers free and looked them over from top to bottom before he handed them over to Bigfoot. My man nodded and passed them to Brian. I watched as my dad's eyes swept over the papers a few times before the tears started to form in his eyes. I didn't wait for confirmation of what I already knew. Instead, I went and wrapped my arms around the man who had raised me and held onto him as he came to grips with the fact that the son he had been raising for four - nearly five - years wasn't his.

"I'm sorry," I whispered into his ear. "I really hoped I was wrong about this."

"Nothing's changed. I'll have to tell him when he's older, but for now, he doesn't need to know." Dad let go of me and looked every man in the eye at least once. "This shit stays in this room unless it is important to what's going on with those bastards who want my land and think they'll get it through my son."

"We will have to let the President of the Mojave Devils in on the fact that the kid is not related to you biologically. It eliminates any claim they think they'll have on your land."

"Does this mean everything can go back to normal?" Dad asked.

"For you and your brothers, I hope so. It doesn't change the fact that Sammy killed two of their men or that Diego Rivera has a hard-on for your daughter."

"You could have phrased that better, babe," I chastised my man.

He shrugged because he honestly didn't care about sugar-coating the truth, not even for my dad.

"What about Colleen?" he asked. "What if she comes back for him?"

"That won't happen," Baffle informed him.

"But he's not mine. He has other family out there. What if-"

I cut my dad off. "We went over this the other day, Dad. Whether he's yours biologically or not, you signed his birth certificate. You chose to marry that woman and raise that child without ever questioning if it was your kid or not. Now, you have to continue to take responsibility for him, just as if you had signed up to adopt a kid who doesn't share your blood because you are all he has. We are all he has. Obviously, the rest of his family is evil, and we'll never know for sure who his father is. He knows that you're his dad and I'm his sister and Josh and Brady are his uncles though. If you can't handle that, you let me know and I'll tell him you had an accident and can't care for him. I'll do it, but what we're not going to do is throw that kid to the wolves when none of this was his fault."

"Colleen is dead. So, that ship has sailed. We won't turn over a kid to the only blood relation we know of because they'd just send the kid to the cartel to deal with."

"What do you mean send him to the cartel? Why would they want him?"

My dad was painfully naive. "It means they smuggle people to other people who want to purchase them, Dad. He would be sold in one type of slavery or another. Considering his age, you might be able to guess the kind of people who would buy him."

"Over my dead fucking body," he roared.

"That's the spirit," I cheered him on, then mumbled, "Finally!"

23. THE CHALLENGE
BIGFOOT

"I was surprised to receive your request for a meeting," Wrecker said the minute I stepped into the room with him. We both had people outside the building and our VPs beside us for the meeting. Candyman gave Baffle a good once over and then brought his attention firmly back to me as I spoke with his president.

"I don't know why you'd be surprised. Your club came gunning for me. Then you came for my ol' lady."

"As much as it pains me to admit this, we did not sanction a hit on you. Our Road Captain, Whip, thought he would go rogue and prove that he should be the one with this patch on his chest." Wrecker laughed as he tapped his president patch. "Didn't work out too well for him."

"Yet you still send your men to take my ol' lady out because you thought she might have been the one to take him out."

"Didn't do that one, either. Though, it was sanctioned by the Rivera Cartel. Whip was their man, after all."

"It stops now, and before you tell me there's more at play than I understand, I came to disabuse you of that notion."

"Disabuse me, huh? Fancy words for a King."

"It's just a fucking word." I threw the DNA results down in front of him. for him. "See? No familial relation at all." Wrecker and Candyman exchanged a pointed look and then he pushed one finger down on the papers and slid them back to me. "Don't suppose you know who the kid's real father is?"

"Nope. Don't care. We're not going to punish the kid for not having Morton blood, but all the same, it means he does not qualify as an heir for inheritance of the family land."

"I concede that point." Wrecker once again looked at his VP and something passed between them that I didn't much like. "There's still the issue of Three."

"Three what?" I asked.

"Three is a who. He was sent to have a conversation with Colleen Morton and he never returned."

"I suggest you find Colleen and ask her, then."

"Colleen hasn't been seen or heard from in a few days. I don't suppose you know anything about that?"

I stepped back and got ready to leave but made sure to get my point across before I did. "I don't know why everyone you're involved with up and leaves, but it has nothing to do with me. My club doesn't go after women, period."

"Even women who clearly tricked your ol' lady's family?" Wrecker asked.

"Even then. If I knew where she was, I'd hand her over to you. Can't imagine you're too happy knowing she fucked up your plans to take those 56 acres the Mortons own. Do your-selves a favor and find a different pipeline between your clubhouse and the fucking Rivera Cartel. If we see any of you enter New Mexico from this point forward, we will shoot first and ask questions later. You stupidly declared war on my club the minute your club tried to take me out, and you admitted it was a member of your club who did so. As the party who can call for retaliation, understand that you have a debt to pay and this is the only day I'll walk away without killing any Mojave Devil who ends up in my sights."

"Big words for a man who was marked by death," Candyman threatened.

"You want me to change my mind and introduce a new leadership to your club today, asshole?"

"That's enough," Wrecker stated as he ordered his man to stand down. "If we find out your club had anything to do with the death of Three or Colleen Morton, there will be retribution coming from our side, as well."

"I wouldn't hold your breath waiting on that. Then again, I have it on good authority that Colleen wiped out Brian Morton's financials and there's a certain sheriff who went missing within a few days of her. Now, I'm not one to gossip, but I've heard a rumor here and there that the two might have been fucking behind Brian's back for quite some time. Possibly, they were together for the entirety of Colleen's marriage to Brian."

"Is he the father of that kid?" Candyman chomped the words out as if each of them had a flavor and he didn't like the way any of them tasted.

"Don't know. We were going to run a sample, but his place was wiped clean by someone. Not sure how you lot operate, but someone with a meticulous track record for disappearing people made sure that Estes and Colleen

Morton didn't leave any trace of themselves behind to find. Do what you will with that information."

Those little kernels of truth were planted on purpose. The Rivera Cartel were known for their flawless cover ups when they took people who might be missed. It was just enough doubt to plant suspicion in the minds of the Mojaves while not offering too much information that might turn their suspicions back on us. I wanted them at one another's throats. It was imperative that their plans didn't just fall apart, but they crumbled around them and left chaos in their wake. Chaos was easier to deal with because it meant people got sloppy.

"Remind your men they're not to cross into New Mexico."

"Remind yours that Arizona is equally off limits, then." I smirked at Candyman. Wrecker had more than one soldier who wanted to overthrow the man at the top.

"Nope. See, the Kings of Anarchy already have a chapter in Arizona. We have three in Texas, one in Nevada, Colorado, and Utah, and I can go on naming states because we have a chapter in every fucking one of them. Do you know what happens when we consolidate all of our resources and point them toward a common enemy?"

They didn't bother to ask for an answer, so I grinned even wider and gave it to them anyway. "We no longer have an enemy," I threatened. Unlike Candyman's threats, mine were very real. Judging by the faces of the two men across from me, they knew it.

24. FAMILY DYNAMICS

SAMMY

OVER THE NEXT TWO WEEKS, WE UNCOVERED A LOT OF DISTURBING things while I kept my brother at the clubhouse with me. Dad and my two uncles went back home and worked together to clear everything of Colleen's out of his house and mine. He also filed a criminal complaint with the new sheriff, Todd Wilburn. Colleen had been keeping a lot of secrets. Some of them were uncovered by Glitch, who couldn't let things go when he tried to figure out how she was related to the man she called her uncle.

As it turned out, her real name was Sabrina Ginger Graham. My dad married a woman named Colleen Sabrina Carlson. Since she didn't exist, technically my father had never remarried anyone. Still, he filed a complaint with the sheriff that she had stolen all the money from his checking and savings account, the furniture from my house, and she had abandoned her son with him.

As some of the items stolen were mine, I had to go with my father to file the complaints. "I'm sorry, Mr. Morton, but there's nothing we can do about the joint checking and savings."

"Why the hell not?"

"You were married. She had every right to take those things."

"No, she didn't," I argued. "She committed fraud when she married my father using a fake name and under false pretenses. She clearly had a plan to financially decimate my family. Since they were never married, the draining of those accounts was a criminal act, as well."

"They had joint accounts, whether the marriage was legal or not," Sheriff Wilburn argued with me.

"She used her fake identity on those joint accounts, which is a crime, Sheriff. I shouldn't have to tell you how the law works."

He closed his eyes and took a deep breath before letting it out. Then he pulled his hat from his head and set it on his desk before he looked me in the eye again. "You're right. It would appear that everything this woman did was based on an act of fraud, and it all falls in the realm of criminality. We can't even begin to compile charges until we have all the facts lined up. Once we do, we will go before the judge, obtain a warrant, and put out a BOLO on Colleen, Sabrina, or whatever in the hell her real name is."

"We need that in writing for insurance purposes," I demanded. Sheriff Wilburn placed his hat back on his head and gave me a curt nod. "Our administrative assistant will have the information for you to pick up within the next two days."

Two days later, Sheriff Wilburn called Dad and told him they needed to have an in-person conversation. Once again, I was there as the sheriff explained what Glitch had already uncovered. My father's fake wife had a lengthy string of aliases and an even longer string of men who she had swindled out of their money and property over the years. One significant source of note was a wealthy businessman near Snowflake, Arizona who offed himself after he lost fifteen acres of his land and his entire savings account to the bitch. That wasn't the worst of the insult, or the reason he supposedly ate a bullet, though. That piece of property quickly turned into the compound where the Mojave Devils built their clubhouse.

My father, having wised up in the past few weeks, finally used his head to point suspicion in the direction of their motorcycle club. "You don't think they took her, do you? What if she was being forced to do those things?" Dad actually shed a few tears as he asked the sheriff. "Oh God! What if she needed help to escape them and I didn't even notice? I'll admit, I married her because she got pregnant, and I was lonely after Joy passed away. I wasn't the most attentive husband. What if she tried to... I don't know..."

Sheriff Wilburn must have felt sorry for my dad's stellar act. "Mr. Morton, whatever you do now, I don't think blaming yourself is the right road to travel down. If this woman wanted to get help, she had plenty of opportunities. As much as it pains me to admit this, we have every reason to believe she was working with former Sheriff Estes. They disappeared around the same time, but some evidence has come to light that suggested they may have been involved in a romantic relationship. His bank accounts were also cleaned out, but it was done by him, and he did not appear to be under duress."

LATER THAT EVENING, after my father was tucked away in his house, and I had come back to the clubhouse to check on the boys, I ran into Melissa. "Were you here to pick up Hawk?" I asked her.

"No. Josh was needed for something. I'm waiting for him to finish whatever super-secret quest the club has him on."

"Oh, okay. Well..." The polite part of me thought I should say something like, "It was good to see you." The other part of me just left the words hanging at "Well..." I knew eventually, I'd have to try to do better with Melissa for Hawk and Uncle Josh's sake. I had tried, but I was still pissed that she lied to ruin things between Bigfoot and me preemptively. And her only reasoning was selfish bullshit. It was hard to forgive that and impossible to forget.

As we stood there with that singular word hanging in the air between us, Tilly made her way to us. She was headed toward me, so she didn't realize who I was talking to when she invited me, Ryan, Hawk, and Bigfoot to a family dinner. I accepted and when Tilly leaned in to hug me, she finally realized who was standing there.

"Oh, Melissa." Her tone was almost cringey in its awkwardness. "I didn't realize you were standing there. I suppose I could extend the invite to you and Josh, as well."

"I appreciate the immense amount of thought you put into our invite, Tilly, but we'll have to decline as we have dinner plans of our own."

Tilly simply nodded and Melissa looked from me to Bigfoot's mom and back a couple times before she simply walked away. Tilly let out a breath I didn't realize she was holding. Then laughter burst free from her, and I realized she hadn't been holding her breath, she had been trying not to laugh in the face of her grandson's mother.

"Thank God!" she wheezed. "I did not have the strength to share a meal with that insufferable woman today."

I laughed along with her. "She can't be that bad. I mean, she was a bitch when I first met her, but I understood her reasons. Sort of."

Tilly rolled her eyes at my feigned diplomacy. "That woman is a handful and a half. Should have seen her when she was pregnant with Hawk. Lord, but you would have thought she was the only person in the history of the Earth to ever be pregnant or have to give birth. Your poor uncle is in for it if he sticks it out with her."

"He seems happy with her, but then again, Uncle Josh can be a challenge, too."

"Ah, a match made in heaven - or would it be hell?" Tilly pondered as she got the ingredients together from the club's pantry for whatever she was making for dinner.

I laughed at her. "Shop here often?"

Tilly grinned and swatted me away playfully. "Just you wait and see how many extra people come to sit at your table when you start hosting dinners. You'll shop at the clubhouse pantry too, if you're smart. Let these boys pay for their own food. They certainly will eat enough of it."

AFTER DINNER, when everyone sat around the table, full, happy, and pleasantly surrounded by family, Bigfoot got up and reached into his pocket before he got down on one knee in front of me. "Samantha Morton, my sweet angel, my beautiful, sassy avenging angel," he corrected with a laugh as everyone followed suit. "You have been mine since I crashed into your life." I chuckled along with everyone else at that. "We're going to have our stag and hen parties in Vegas next week because the weekend after, we're getting married at the clubhouse." After he got that mouthful of an order out, he shoved a beautiful ring onto my finger, leaned forward and kissed it, then grinned up at me with that wide, knowing smile of his.

Yeah, that gorgeous face of his could get away with a lot. Since he hadn't asked a question, I didn't bother to answer him. I simply asked, "Isn't it a bit too soon?"

He wasn't the one who responded to me. His mother did. "Oh, honey! When the Cardwell men decide they've found the one, they don't leave anything to chance. I'm honestly surprised you're not already married. Crutch had a minister preside over our wedding while I was still passed out cold and couldn't say no to him. That was two weeks after we met."

When I say my jaw dropped, I mean the damn thing literally touched the table. "I'm going to need a story time about that later, Tilly."

Tilly waved me off again as if I was being silly. "Another day, maybe. This is your day! Congratulations, my sweet girl, and welcome to the family. We're so proud to have you as one of our own."

Ryan hopped up and down in his seat as he tapped Hawk on the shoulder repeatedly. "Are we budders now?"

Hawk looked to his dad for an answer because he was obviously confused by the question too. "That's a complicated answer, now isn't it?" My new fiancé teased me. All of the adults started to laugh until Hawk spoke up.

"If I'm your brother, then Sammy is my sister," Hawk mused.

"Fuck!" Bigfoot hissed as I threw my head back and laughed at the situation Melissa had been so afraid of.

"Lord help these children to one day understand," Tilly prayed.

25. BACHELOR PARTY
BIGFOOT

"The women took Sammy to an all-male review," Dime told me as he slung another shot back.

"What's that mean?" I asked as I pushed the dancer away from my lap for the third time. If she tried to sit on my dick again, she'd find herself laid out on the floor, maybe missing teeth. I wouldn't hit her, but I would make certain that she hit the floor instead of my lap. It was bad enough glitter seemed to drip off of her and glue itself to me every time she got too close.

"It means that your woman is probably humping up on some young stud who won't have a problem pulling his dick out of those tiny little banana hammocks they wear on stage."

"No!" I yelled as I stood up and surprise, surprise the bitch who couldn't take no for an answer tipped over and fell flat on her ass.

It didn't take me long to find out where the girls took my woman for her hen party. It took even less time for me to show up there and find my woman parked on a chair, center stage, wearing a sash that declared her to be "The Bride".

I was going to take her over my knee as soon as I got her somewhere private. The only reason I'd wait for that was because there was no fucking way any of the dancers or staff in the joint were going to watch as my woman took pleasure in her spanking. And she would. She absolutely would.

The man in front of her dropped his pants and waved his dick in her face. I charged the stage like a fucking bull who saw the red cape swing. "Hell to the fuck no!" I bellowed as I ran to free my woman who would never voluntarily allow herself to be tied to a chair in front of an audience. It didn't matter that she was laughing hysterically. I imagined she was only laughing at the asshole's tiny size compared to me. "Sammy!" I called and she finally tilted her head my way. Her eyes bulged at the sight of me. "You better get away from that fucker, right now!"

"I am," She stopped to hiccup. "Tied to a chair, Bigfoot!"

"Why in the hell did you allow yourself to be tied to a chair?"

"Tradition!" she cried out to me as all the women around threw their heads back and howled to a moon that didn't exist because it was two o'clock on a fucking Thursday. We just happened to be in Vegas where anything goes around the clock.

"Fuck that! Having a naked man dance on you is not a tradition we're going to uphold."

"So, you weren't at a strip club with some bitch throwing her tits in your face as she rained glittered down all over you?" Sammy tried to eye me suspiciously, but the amount of liquor she consumed made her giggle for some reason. Then she started singing Umbrella by Rhianna at the top of her lungs. "When the sun shines, we shine together..." It was... not attractive... at all. My woman couldn't sing to save her life or mine. It was a good thing she was a crack shot with a gun.

"Come on baby, that's different, and besides I pushed that bitch off me like three times. You're grinning up at this idiot like he has a bigger dick than me and we know that's not true."

Sammy threw her head back and laughed, then immediately sat forward again. "Whoa! Head rush!"

Finally, I reached the stage. Fucking crazy ass women kept getting in my way and feeling me up. "If you know what's good for you, this is the part where you run away," my fiancé warned the dancer. I climbed up onto the stage and picked my woman up, chair and all, as the dancer heeded her warning and launched himself as far from me as he could get. Unfortunately for the poor bastard, he flung himself into the crowd of horny women and I didn't think he'd make it up for air before I walked my Sammy down the aisle to marry me. Wait... No, before she walked down the aisle to marry me next weekend. I was pretty sure her dad had to walk her down that aisle. None of that mattered. The dancer was a goner, and I didn't help traitors.

I managed to get my woman back to the private rooms, slipped the bouncer a few hundred bucks and he let us in. "Thirty minutes," he cautioned.

"Only need about three," I stated confidently.

He laughed the whole way down the hall and Sammy giggled at me too. "Aren't you going to untie me?"

"Not a fucking chance. You want to uphold tradition,

baby. I'm the man who is gonna dance for you." It was possible that I was a little drunk, too. Especially since it felt like I was already dancing, but I didn't think the music had started yet.

I didn't get to dance to for my woman because while I was trying to figure out if the music was on, my woman managed to get herself untied and then she let out a battle cry to end all battle cries as she tackled me to the sticky as fuck floor and slammed her mouth down on my mine. "Did I ever tell you that I love you?" she asked when she pulled back.

"Nope."

"I do."

"You're supposed to save those words for our wedding." She giggled again. "Sammy?"

"Yeah, big guy?"

"I love you, too.

We both woke up the next day with a killer as fuck hangover and loaded up on the plane back home with everyone else who was a little worse for the wear. "Baffle?" I called out when I noticed he was missing. After realizing no one had seen him that morning, I pulled my phone out and dialed his number.

"Baffle," he groaned into the phone.

"Hey man, we all boarded our flight already. Where the fuck are you?"

"Uh, shit man. I have something I need to deal with. I'll be back before the wedding, so don't replace me as your best man."

"What the fuck is so important?"

"I'll fill you in when I get back."

"You need backup?"

"Nah. At least, I don't think so." Baffle hung up just as the flight attendant came around and asked me to put my phone on airplane mode for takeoff.

26. WEDDING SURPRISE

SAMMY

BIGFOOT WAS FREAKING OUT THE MORNING OF OUR WEDDING. I knew because I could hear him shouting the clubhouse down looking for his best man. "I hope Baffle gets here soon," I muttered to my soon-to-be mother-in-law.

"Me too or that boy will be in a world of hurt when he does show up." She eyed some of the women who were sequestered with me. As if the "can't see the bride before the wedding" applied to all of them too. "Roxy is hoping your wedding will make Baffle realize it's time to settle down."

I hated to break it to either of them, but I was fairly certain Baffle wasn't interested in Roxy. Not as anything more than an occasional fuck buddy at best. Then again, I didn't really know because the man played his cards tight to his chest. The only person who stood a chance at guessing something like that was my fiancé.

"I'm here fucker, can you pipe down before you raise the dead?"

"That's not funny!" Bigfoot declared as I peeked out the door and watched the two men embrace in that weird back slap, half hug hybrid thing they did. There was a woman staring adoringly up at Baffle from just off to his side. As soon as he pulled back from Bigfoot, my man asked, "Who is this?"

"Funny story," Baffle nervously chuckled as he admitted that. "This is Nell, my wife."

"Your what?" Bigfoot asked, clearly shocked by the development.

"Your what?" A woman screeched from somewhere beside me. My ear started to ring as all the women flooded out of the room we'd been holed-up in. "You had better be fucking joking, Patrick fucking Mendoza! We were supposed to get married!"

"You were engaged?" The woman who Baffle claimed to be married to asked in a soft voice.

"No. I was not engaged. I wasn't even dating anyone before I left."

"You know good and damn well we were always supposed to end up together!" Roxy shouted. When Baffle didn't so much as blink at her assertion, she turned her claws on the seemingly meek woman who was wrapped under Baffle's arm. "You conniving little whore!" she shouted before she launched herself at Nell.

Bigfoot caught her before she could make contact and bellowed. "Punchy, you better get over here and get your daughter! I am not putting my wedding off because she can't handle reality when it hits her."

That was a little cold, but then again, I didn't ever remember seeing Roxy by Baffle's side the way that he had Nell tucked against him. There was a bit of a scuffle and eventually the woman was escorted out and the music started up that was supposed to signal my walk down the aisle.

I glanced around and was only mildly disappointed when I didn't see my dad anywhere. Our arrival back at the clubhouse was greeted with the news that Brian never showed up to collect Ryan from Bigfoot's mother. She ended up keeping him with Hawk the whole time we were gone. Neither Josh nor Brady knew where he was either. My heart hurt for poor little Ryan. We already had to explain to him that his mother was gone, and now my dad had pulled a runner and didn't even bother to stick around long enough to walk me down the aisle.

Brady moved in about the same time Crutch came to my side. "Looks like you have a choice, young lady," Crutch offered.

"Please, don't be offended, but I want Uncle Brady to be the one to give me away. He's been the most like my dad since my mom passed away."

"No explanations needed. I just didn't want to see my beautiful daughter-in-law left in the lurch when she was in need of an escort."

"Thank you, Crutch."

"Anytime, darlin."

I took Brady's arm, and he guided me to the makeshift aisle. Before I knew it, he offered my hand over to Bigfoot who looked at me like I was the best thing he had ever seen.

We said our vows; whatever Smooth made us repeat since he was the one to get ordained to marry us. I couldn't remember a bit of it because I was focused on the man who had crashed into my life and turned it upside down in the best way possible. At a time when it felt like my family was coming apart at the seams, he was there to stitch the ripped pieces back together for me.

As we danced our first dance together, we watched as Punchy made his way to Baffle. There was a lot of pointing and arguing before Baffle finally lost his temper with the man. "There's nothing to explain, old man. Roxy and I were never even dating, let alone in a serious relationship."

"You telling me my daughter was just your fuck buddy?"

"I'm telling you that I drunkenly slept with her one fucking time three years ago. Other than that, we've only ever been good friends. The best of friends at times. I don't know where she got this fantasy of marrying me stuck in her head, but that is Roxy's problem not mine, and I won't have you disrespecting my wife like this. I brought her home to meet my club family and so far she's been left feeling like an unwelcome mistake. I won't fucking have it, not in my own home!"

Crutch made his way to them and finally got Punchy to back down. As he took him back out of the clubhouse, Bigfoot snatched my hand and pulled me back toward his office.

"Where are we going?" I whispered as we sneaked away.

"We're going to find our favorite supply closet because I don't want to watch everyone's fucked-up soap opera drama when I could be fucking my wife instead." I giggled.

"We could have just as easily made a break for it upstairs to our room."

He shook his head. "Nope. Someone would have noticed us on the stairs. In here," He closed the office door behind us and locked it, "we can disappear to a place only a few people know exists."

I giggled again because the majority of the club knew about the cave system beneath the clubhouse property. While part of it was used for the grow house operation, the other part was used as an escape tunnel in the case of an emergency.

"Wait, is Colleen still down here?" I asked because no one had ever given me a real answer as to what happened to her. At one point, I assumed she was dead because I'd been told repeatedly that I didn't have to worry about her ever again. Still, there was a part of me that needed to know.

"This better not ruin our wedding fuck," Bigfoot lamented. Then he took both of my hands and pulled me into the supply closet where we fucked the day I tortured Colleen. If you could call it torture, since it only took being stabbed twice and smacked with a knife for her to cooperate.

"You know how you stuck her with those two knives?" my husband asked me.

"Yeah, of course, I'm the one that put them in her thighs."

"Well, the second one nicked an artery or something. Dime went to pull the knife out after they got all the information they could from her, and it started to spurt blood everywhere. The guys who were still down here with her were kind of shocked that it sprayed like a thick fountain, and no one thought to stop it. By the time they got something to tie it off and put pressure on the damn thing, it was too late."

I laughed so hard it hurt. "So, in other words, the damage was done, so they watched her bleed out?"

"I guess, if you want to put it that way, sure." Bigfoot hedged.

I rolled my eyes at him and then leaned up on my tip toes to kiss his lips. "I appreciate you trying to protect me or whatever that was you were trying to do, but there is no need to lie to me ever. You tell everything to me straight and we will never have a problem. Got it?"

"Got it," Bigfoot agreed. "Now get naked because I need to fuck my wife."

PLAYLIST

The music that inspired some of the scenes in this book is on the harder side of rock (some of it).

You can find the playlist on Apple Music:
Apple Music Hard Rock.
Link:
https://music.apple.com/us/playlist/weekend-warriors/pl.
a539367ed1ec4df995d2ef01df68e5eb

Includes various titles from the following bands/musicians:
Ozzy Osborne
Linkin Park
Avenged Sevenfold
Ghost
Slipknot
King Diamond
Guns-N-Roses
Soundgarden
Seether

PLAYLIST

Skillet

Foo Fighters

Bring Me the Horizon

Disturbed

Volbeat

Spiritbox

Saving Abel

Metallica

Sleep Token

Iron Maiden

Killswitch Engage

Audioslave

Rammstein

Halestorm

Rage Against the Machine

Dorothy

And many more...

Kings of Anarchy MC: New Mexico Book 2
By Christine Michelle

About the Book:

Nell

I married a stranger.

That stranger happened to be the vice president of a motorcycle club and not the fluffy bunny type of biker either. My new husband was part of a club that had one hell of an outlaw reputation. He also had a close female friend back home with her own plan to marry him one day. She refused to take "No" for an answer.

There were signs from the very beginning that this was not meant to work out. Waking up married to a stranger in Vegas should have been the first. Still, the way he made my heart race faster with just one smoldering look was reason enough to give it the old college try, even if I ended with nothing more than a broken heart in the end.

Baffle

Our start wasn't conventional.

Thanks to my family and close friends, her introduction to my life was downright hostile.

Maybe I was a selfish man, but I refused to let her go. In spite of everything we faced, there was just something about Nell that kept me coming back for more and made me unwilling to give her up.

ALSO BY CHRISTINE MICHELLE

CHRISTINE MICHELLE

Kings of Anarchy MC: New Mexico

Property of Bigfoot

Aces High MC – Dakotas

Dancing with Danger · Whiskey Tango Foxtrot · The Restart and the Remedy

Aces High MC – Charleston

The Other Princess · A Love So Hard · The Princess and the Prospect · The Killing Ride · A Twist of Fate · Everlasting · A Year and a Day ·The Broken Beginning – Part One ·The Broken Beginning – Part Two

Aces High MC – Tallahassee

Crushed

Aces High MC – Sierra High

Walker · Trouble

Aces High MC – Cedar Falls

Redemption Weather · Proven · Smoke and the Flame · Redemption Duet Box Set

S.H.E. MC

Angel Girl · JoJo · Keys

Death Viewers

Breathless

Upper YA Titles

The Voodoo Follies (PNR)

Catch a Falling Star (Dystopian Romance)

ANNE STORM

Savage Vipers MC

Wait For Me · Devastate Me · Surprise Me · Baby Me

Loved for the Holidays

Cupid Broke My Heart · Ghosted by Texas · Resolving Rumors

Cheating Hearts Series

The Homewrecker's Fate · The Regrettable Mistake

ABOUT THE AUTHOR

Christine Michelle also writes under the name Anne Storm.
Anne Storm's books:
Dark romance/subjects with major triggers
Christine Michelle's books:
(mild) MC Romance, Rock Star Romance, and other
Contemporary Romance
Paranormal Fantasy & Romance
If you want to learn more about Christine, her books, or her
crazy adventures into the wilderness, you can find out more
through the following links:
Website & Newsletter sign up:
www.moonlitdreams.org
Signing up for the newsletter also gets you first option at
future Beta reading and ARC (advanced reader copy)
giveaway opportunities!
**Universal links to everything
(social media, book links, and more)**
https://linktr.ee/christinemichelle

facebook.com/M00nlitDreams
instagram.com/christinemichelle_annestorm
tiktok.com/@christine.michelle.books

www.ingramcontent.com/pod-product-compliance
Lightning Source LLC
Chambersburg PA
CBHW031223260626
47169CB00007B/2170